About the author

Dr Keith Fisher has been a chemist all his working life and has lived in several countries.

He was born in 1940 in Birmingham during the bombing. He grew up in Birmingham and, after passing the eleven-plus, went to grammar school in Smethwick.

After leaving grammar school, he went to work in a couple of laboratories and did his degree in chemistry part-time. He then went to Canada to start his postgraduate degree, which he finished at the University of London in England.

After gaining his PhD, he went to America for five years and had several teaching appointments at universities. After returning to the UK he took up a post at the University of Lagos, later followed by a post at the University of Khartoum in the Sudan. Thirteen years in Africa were followed by two years in Canada and finally, in 1989, he came to Australia.

EXPATS IN THE SUDAN

Keith Fisher

EXPATS IN THE SUDAN

Vanguard Press

VANGUARD PAPERBACK

© Copyright 2020
Keith Fisher

The right of Keith Fisher to be identified as author of
this work has been asserted by him in accordance with the
Copyright, Designs and Patents Act 1988.

All Rights Reserved

No reproduction, copy or transmission of this publication
may be made without written permission.
No paragraph of this publication may be reproduced,
copied or transmitted save with the written permission of the
publisher, or in accordance with the provisions
of the Copyright Act 1956 (as amended).

Any person who commits any unauthorised act in relation to
this publication may be liable to criminal
prosecution and civil claims for damages.

A CIP catalogue record for this title is
available from the British Library.

ISBN 978 1 784659 08 0

*Vanguard Press is an imprint of
Pegasus Elliot MacKenzie Publishers Ltd.*
www.pegasuspublishers.com

First Published in 2020

**Vanguard Press
Sheraton House Castle Park
Cambridge England**

Printed & Bound in Great Britain

Dedication

To my lovely second wife, Ela, who I met in Khartoum.

This is a work of fiction. Names, characters, businesses, places, events and incidents are either the products of the author's imagination or used in a fictitious manner. Any resemblance to actual persons, living or dead, or actual events is purely coincidental.

Contents

The Sudan club 11

Khartoum, Home 15

A Gift from Burglars 30

The Left-Handed Sudanese 46

Juba 59

Khartoum Trilogy 73

Aid to Africa 73

Sent Home 104

Kathy's Story 113

Found in Kenya 141

Sharia 166

An Unfortunate Insult 201

Getting the Bumps Knocked Out 222

The Sudan club

Khartoum is a city surrounded by desert; Sudan was at the time the largest country in Africa (during the period I was there 1980-86) and yet this capital was relatively small. Like all African cities it was growing but the lack of infrastructure slowed the process; it would take a war to change the growth. In summer, May to September average daytime temperatures of forty degrees centigrade were not uncommon and the best time in Khartoum was December and January when daytime temperatures could be over thirty degrees. Rain was a very rare occurrence; there might be a few showers in July or August and occasionally in September. Even clouds in the sky were a rarity.

The confluence of the White and Blue Nile made Khartoum an important trading centre and this had been the case for centuries. Most of the population were Arabs, mainly Sunni Muslims but there were also Shia and other sects such as Dervish. The Dervishes made their presence felt at weekends in Omdurman. Like any trading centre there were lots of other nationalities, principally Egyptian, Lebanese, Greek and Syrian. After Gordon's death, at the hands of the Mahdi's followers, the British forces under Kitchener took over control of the Sudan. Sudan became a British-Egyptian protectorate and the British set up the civil service and had a standing army mainly based in Khartoum.

In 1956 Sudan was declared an independent country with a Sudanese civilian government. The British and Egyptian armed forces were no longer needed and their numbers drastically reduced. At a later date the cathedral in Khartoum was converted into government offices and several properties belonging to foreigners were confiscated. One of the properties was Greek owned and these premises were converted into the Sudan Club.

When the British had been in power, they set up three clubs, as the British do. One was for senior civil servants and high-ranking army officers. The second was for lower rank civil servants and army officers. The third club was for ordinary soldiers. No one ever told me about the commercial Brits but I guess their 'station' put them in one of the three clubs. With a large reduction of civil servants and the army, the Sudanese government decided that one British club was all that was required. They made membership for this club for British passport holders only; the rumour was that they wanted to keep the Sudanese from mixing with the previous rulers. It was also rumoured that several of the staff were reporting to the Sudanese authorities about the goings on of these now foreigners. One or two Sudanese could join as their spouses were British. The premises of the British club were a confiscated property of a Greek trader.

At about the same time the Sudanese government set up other clubs, I think on confiscated property. There was an Armenian, a Coptic and a Syrian club, I think the American club came later. At a later date the Sudanese government relaxed the rule of British passport holders only, to allow ten percent of the members to be Commonwealth citizens. This quota was almost always full and so temporary membership was introduced. Many incoming members commented on the anachronism of a club for British only, but no one had the courage (or temerity) to approach the Sudanese government to change the rules.

I came to the Sudan in 1980 and immediately joined the Sudan Club; my experience in Nigeria dictated an urgency. Not knowing much Arabic made social life difficult and it was easy to use English in social settings there. The club was very close to the centre of Khartoum and it was like a tranquil oasis. The facilities were good, the food was English 'style' and drinks were a reasonable price. The snooker room was an attraction and the swimming pool a definite plus when children visited from the UK. The fees were a little steep but worth it. After a year or so I joined the committee and later became the secretary. When Sharia came, I was secretary and had a lot of problems in dealing with members. I later became president of the club but with Sharia in force the club was on the way down, a sad state of affairs. Gatherings without booze are un-British. We tried to keep traditional celebrations going but it was difficult. I invited two Russian ladies to a Burns Night which could not happen without a tipple of home-made 'stuff'. The club had a good stock of booze, but it was all locked up in the store — such a waste! When I was leaving Sudan in 1986 the club was on its last legs, such a shame. I later found out that the Greek family had retrieved their property.

Khartoum, Home

Faded glory, no maintenance, hot desert sand, cruel sun and a seemingly uncaring population: urban decay Khartoum style but Dave loved it. Strolling down Ghamhouria Street at noon was no pleasure for most Europeans, but for Dave it was a pleasant ritual. Weaving his way through the crowd, avoiding the merchandise lining the pavement and dodging the aggressive traders and beggars, Dave looked completely out of place. A stocky little Welshman, a long way from home, but this was Dave's home. Khartoum had been his home for more than thirty years. Aberystwyth was a place he visited once a year to see his mother. He hated the cold and the rain; in Khartoum it was never cold and it almost never rained. He loved Khartoum but could he afford to live here any longer? Why would he go and where would he go?

Over thirty years earlier Dave had arrived at Khartoum Airport, a dump in the desert was Dave's first impression. Arriving close to midnight on a day in September had been a shock to Dave's system. Leaving a wet cold morning in London he had stepped off the plane into a dust storm in a furnace. Inappropriately dressed (in a suit and tie), he was sweating profusely waiting for the immigration officers to arrive. When they showed up, they all looked like they had just awoken from sleep. They had probably had a snooze, who would not in this heat, thought Dave. The baggage took an interminable time to arrive and Dave was wondering whether his bladder, or even his whole body, could take the strain. The drinks on the plane had been free and Dave was not one to miss a 'freebie'. Dave was soon to learn that his bladder was never too full to need urgent emptying in Khartoum. When in the UK the reverse was the case, a couple of beers and he was visiting the urinal. Dave also noticed that he could have bought his duty-free much cheaper in Khartoum than what he had paid in the UK.

Dave had just received his M.A. in English and had applied for many jobs; the University of Khartoum had offered him a job as a lecturer. His supervisor had written him a good recommendation, even though he thought Dave's chances of getting an offer were slim. So his supervisor had been surprised at Dave's offer and when he learned of the pay and conditions he was a little jealous. Dave was going to one of the best universities in Africa and the supplement from the British government made the salary almost as good as that of a professor in a British university. Dave was to get free accommodation and three months leave and paid passage home every year. As the news of Dave's job spread, many of his peers and several of his lecturers were filled with jealousy. What surprised him was their lack of knowledge of where Khartoum was in relation to 'the rest of the world'. Dave had been consulting maps and history books long before his offer, but nothing had prepared him for the reality. Maps showed the place; history was about wars, but there was little about living conditions and daily life.

Reality was a September night a thousand miles south of Cairo, hot and anxiously waiting for his suitcase. The luggage came and although everyone else seemed to be having a problem with customs, Dave was not even asked to open his suitcase. Everyone seemed to smile at him. It was unnerving; this could not happen at Gatwick or Heathrow. Dave pushed his way through the good natured crowd to the exit. His bags hit several people and they apologised before he could. A couple of the apologies were in very well-spoken English and he started to wonder how he could live up to his M.A. The heat was getting to him. How could it be so hot at midnight? Where was the person who was supposed to meet him? What was the Arabic word for university and where was he going to sleep?

Emerging from the terminal he did notice a slight drop in temperature, but it was still bloody hot. Dave looked around at the brown dusty landscape, at least what he could see of it. It was so different to what he had expected but he should have known; this was the edge of the desert. There were crowds of people, battered old taxis and green uniformed police with pistols strapped to their waists. He noticed that most of the police had no laces in their boots and, more disturbingly, there was no white face in sight. His instincts told him he had to be careful; he could lose a bag or a wallet in this place. He was totally wrong. He was in probably the safest capital in Africa and possibly the friendliest to the white man north of the equator. The smiles were not deceptive, they were genuine; the stares were not aggressive just inquisitive; black was just their skin colour, white was his. Later Dave would meet Sudanese who were as white as he and then he would learn that skin colour did matter.

No one was at the airport to meet him and after about ten minutes he decided he would have to find his own way to the university. He approached a taxi driver, but the man had no English and Dave had no Arabic. It then dawned on him that the people apologizing to him as he hit them with his bags were educated Sudanese, not the average taxi driver. Dave looked back at the terminal and realized that the good-natured English-speaking crowd had gone home and he was left with smiling uneducated Sudanese. Inwardly Dave laughed at himself; here he was a master of English in an uncomprehending crowd of well-meaning Arabs. He cursed himself for not learning a bit of Arabic (he did not even know the word for university) before coming to this alien environment. He had concentrated on the geography but neglected the language.

The Bank of Khartoum sign caught Dave's eye — maybe they could help him. The bank was just closing when he hurried to the door. His bags had seemed so light in the UK, but they were a real burden in this terrible heat. Many hands had offered help but he had declined their help because he was suspicious of their motives.

In the bank he changed ten pounds and found that he received less than ten Sudanese pounds. Of course, he had not checked the currency tables before leaving the UK but he still felt cheated. The bank clerk spoke excellent English and told Dave the Arabic word for university. He then took Dave out to find a suitable taxi driver who was given instructions to take Dave to a university hostel. Dave looked back at the bank; it was open and unprotected, and here was the clerk negotiating with a taxi driver. Dave thanked the clerk who waved at him as the taxi drove off. He then strolled back to the bank; to Dave that was remarkable. He vowed to learn Arabic as quickly as possible but even thirty years later he had not completely mastered the language. Life was to be eventful in Khartoum but not as challenging as those first few days.

The drive to the university guest house seemed to be very long and nearly ended in disaster. Turning from a lit street, with potholes as big as small cars, into an unlit unpaved street the taxi had gone into a ditch. The driver and Dave both got out surveying the problem, but the moon seemed to be out that night. Although it was dark, they could see the problem but then the dogs started barking. This unnerved Dave making him look into each dark area. The taxi driver had missed the turn and the front wheel had gone towards, but not quite into, the ditch. With Dave's help pushing and the driver reversing they were able to get out of the ditch and could proceed. They only travelled about one hundred yards down this street to the front of the hostel. Of course, at this time of night, the gates were locked and there were no lights in the compound. The driver started banging on the gates for what seemed about ten minutes and Dave was getting worried that the police might come and arrest them for disturbing the peace. Dave later found out that he need not have worried, although the night watchman might have been arrested for keeping the hawaga (white man) waiting. Finally, there was a grunt from inside the gate and it was opened by a tall, very black man with a rather large knife in his belt. Alan looked at the knife and hoped he never came across the man and his knife unsheathed.

The guest house only had one room left and that only had a fan. Dave entered the pitch-black room and finally found the light switch; he started the fan and flopped onto the bed. That was the last memory of his first night in Khartoum, and when he awoke in the morning, he was hot but not really sweating. He did have a thirst though, and his throat was so dry.

Through the cracks in the window blind he could see it was very bright outside. He adjusted his eyes as he pulled back the blind; the light was almost blinding, there was not a cloud in the sky and the sky was so blue.

Dave wanted to rush outside and get a bit of that sun but first he needed to find a drink. He opened his door and entered a small corridor which lead to a sort of kitchen where there was a small fridge making a terrible noise. Opening the fridge, he found a couple of bottles of water and in the cupboard, he found some small glasses (he was later to find out these were used for tea). He quickly finished one bottle of water and resisted the temptation to drink the second bottle. He refilled the first bottle with water and put it back in the fridge before deciding to take a look outside.

Oh, it was hot and dusty outside! The house was in a walled compound, and after a couple of minutes in the sun Dave decided the indoors might be best. It was a wise choice as only an idiot or a European, tries to absorb the sun's energy for a prolonged time in Khartoum.

As he was about to go indoors the gate opened and a tall man in a white flowing robe walked in with the greeting, "Welcome to Khartoum or, more correctly, North Khartoum, Mr. Dave. We heard you had arrived and we apologize for not picking you up, but the driver fell asleep. I am Hashim, secretary of the English department, come to take you to the university".

Dave came to know Hashim very well in the next few years. Those first few days were hectic; he moved to a much nicer guest house in Khartoum 2 (one of the best districts in Khartoum) where there were a few other

Europeans, he joined the payroll and obtained a bank account. Hashim was invaluable.

Dave's first weeks in his first real job were enlightening; work was easy but living was more difficult. To get to work he had to try to catch a bus or a taxi or a box. A box was a covered utility vehicle with a couple of bench seats in the back, two or three people could sit in the cabin with the driver, and in the back were six people seated and others standing or hanging onto the sides. The buses were not much better, with metal seats, generally no windows, and a floor of metal that seemed to burn through the soles of your shoes. Dave made an early mistake of sitting near the window on a bus and putting his arm on the window ledge; he burnt his arm!

The hostel did not provide food and so Dave had to go to the market to buy what he needed. That was a hassle. The market was always crowded and, of course, hot and then you had to haggle over prices and Dave was not a good haggler. Slowly he learned some 'souk Arabic' and found breakfast at the Uni Staff Club was edible.

As time went by in his first year, he did contemplate leaving but the money was good, and his job took up little of his time. Only the living was difficult. Then he found the Sudan Club. This was the British club formed after independence in 1956. It was near the centre of Khartoum within walking distance of the uni, a long walk in the sun. One day at lunch time he walked there and asked the gate boy if he could go in and find a friend, the gate boy obliged, and Dave found the office and got a proposal form. He then had to find a proposer and seconder and produce a passport to show he was British. The fees were a bit steep, but when he saw the dinner menu with fish and chips or bangers and mash, he was sold. At lunch time the bar was full, and he had no problem getting a proposer and seconder. In a way, joining the Sudan Club had a very great influence on Dave deciding to stay in Khartoum.

Dave had students keen and willing to learn; they knew that English was the way to get on in the outside world and even in Khartoum. Dave was amazed that in this hostile environment lived a friendly placid people. The whole city, actually three towns Omdurman, Khartoum North and Khartoum, seemed to be full of well-wishers, almost do-gooders. People were so good to him he thought that some time the spell would break. The mean, difficult people were the expatriates; they seemed to want to place everyone on a ladder, in some sort of pecking order. Later he was to find out that the locals also had a pecking order, but that took longer to see.

The first year was the hardest but as leave time approached, he started to get excited. Nine months had passed quite quickly and now he was back to the UK for three months. He had saved money from his salary and there was money in the bank from the British government, so now he felt rich. When the time came to leave, he was given air tickets and three month's salary in advance; London awaited then Wales.

Three months was too long; he became bored and even longed to get back to Khartoum. He decided to have a couple of weeks in Greece on his way back and visit a few islands. Greece seemed to be a sort of middle ground between the UK and Sudan, and the next year he decided to spend two weeks in the UK and the rest in Greece. He was fascinated with Crete and vowed that was the place he would spend most time. As each year passed, his life revolved around nine months in Khartoum, two weeks in the UK and the rest in Greece (mostly in Crete). The nine months in Khartoum was no problem as the teaching became easier with each year, and his Arabic was improving so living became easier too.

As the years passed, he noticed the change in the members of the Sudan Club. When he had arrived, many were 'ex-colonials' who had come from Kenya, Zambia or Rhodesia. Their attitude was 'we are gods to the natives'. They did not treat the Sudanese badly but with condescension. As time passed, they were being replaced by the money makers and a few socialist do-gooders who knew nothing about the Sudanese social structure but thought it had to be changed. The locals did not change till about 1980.

Dave's position had been supported by the British government until 1979. The British Government decided that English was not a priority. The allowance had not been excessive, but it went straight into his English bank account. It was useful when on leave, but in Khartoum the Sudanese salary was sufficient for a good bachelor life. Dave did not smoke (although cigarettes were very cheap in Sudan), he also only drank in moderation and did not have a girlfriend. He was not really a ladies' man neither was he a man's man; Dave was sort of sexually neutral. He had always turned down open invitations on Khartoum street corners from men in white trousers; he also dodged fairly explicit invitations at expatriate cocktail parties. There were also some hints from expatriate ladies, but he ignored them. Dave's sexual orientation was not understood and even his mother suspected something. He partially satisfied her by intimating that he had a girlfriend in Greece and that was why he spent so much time there. The expatriate community was not so easily satisfied and rumours surfaced frequently about Dave's 'sexual purpose in life'. He always weathered the storms, and was quite adept at deflecting the 'problem'. He often left the club early in the evening before the real drinking started and tongues loosened. He wondered why all the expatriate males were 'raving studs', homosexuals or just plain 'nutters'. The women were not much better. One or two of the married women had pursued him and some of the others seemed to be 'problem children of the first order'. Even in Greece he was known as a loner. He visited the same island every year and was either alone or in the company of a married couple both of whom seemed to be equally friendly towards him. Dave was such a friendly guy that the hotel and bar owners started to protect him from the advances of locals of either sex. Dave was no saint, but he was treated in Greece and Sudan with such respect that he wondered whether he was divinely protected.

After 1980 the Sudanese pound started to be devalued and Dave was forced to look at his life more realistically. Living became harder and the people seemed to become more aggressive. Inflation was rising and it was biting into everyone's lifestyle. His vacations became more expensive and even though Greece was relatively cheap he could not stay there for two months. The Sudanese pound was collapsing and although he was promoted to senior lecturer the increase in pay could not keep up with inflation. His friends were leaving, and the university was being denuded of expatriates. Dave's monetary problems were minor compared to those of his Sudanese colleagues; they had families to support. Almost without exception his fellow lecturers at the university were trying to get jobs out of the Sudan. Sabbaticals, leaves of absence, secondments, these became the words of conversation in the staff common room. Saudi Arabia, the Gulf States or even Libya were attracting the best Sudanese; it was demoralizing. He found himself filling in for other lecturers, doing more work at exam time and even monitoring other lecturers' exams. None of it was a real burden but a constant reminder of a deteriorating position.

The expatriate community was also on the move, the old stalwarts were dying out or being replaced by 'get rich quick merchants' or construction foremen. If the old colonialists had been difficult to live with, the new lot were impossible. They talked only about money — even the aid workers were mainly interested in money. The old colonials never passed up a chance of making money, but it did not seem to be their only object in life. The old colonials had a condescending attitude to the Sudanese but the newcomers seemed to actively dislike or abuse them. Dave was continually biting his tongue in the club listening to new arrivals telling him how to treat (or more often mistreat) the locals. Dave heard it all and tried arguing a few times but generally his experience had taught him to remove himself from the company and go home.

When Sharia law was introduced, he expected half the expatriate population to leave immediately, preferably the ones he disliked the most. The restrictions on alcohol did not affect Dave too much, but the Sudan Club became very quiet for a while once no alcohol could be served. After a brief period when everyone stayed at home or left, he found some drifting back to the club. Now the conversation was almost exclusively about how to make wine or beer or where to go to the next party. As Dave was a bit of a loner and did not make his own alcoholic drinks he was rarely invited to parties, but he did get to sample a few of the homebrew efforts. Dave decided he could wait for leave rather than get into the game of palate bashing. He did occasionally get hold of a bottle of 'Ethiopian Gin' on the black market but the Mellotti, as it was called, was no substitute for the real thing (even a low-grade Metaxas were preferable).

Dave was able to supplement his salary with some tutoring of the children of rich Sudanese. Two of his early graduates had done very well and one had a son and the other a daughter; Dave tutored them both. They gave him good money and food was laid on for his visits. He was treated very well and could have interesting conversations when the tutoring was finished. These two former students had plenty of contacts who all had children they wanted to learn 'proper' English, and they wanted their children to go to British universities. He could make more than his salary tutoring but he had to limit his workload as he often felt so tired in the evening; the climate was getting to him.

Finally, one of Dave's oldest friends at the university decided to leave. They sat together in the staff club before leaving, reviewing old times and looking to the future. Inevitably the conversation turned to money. When they had both arrived the Sudanese pound had been worth $2.40, more than the British pound, and now you were lucky to get $1 for two Sudanese pounds. Dave had to agree with his friend that life was now very difficult in Sudan, but Dave vowed to stay as long as he could or until they kicked him out or stopped paying him. As he wished his friend goodbye, he realized what he had was worth more than money. He was a king (in Khartoum), albeit a poor one, why abdicate in time of difficulty?

Where could he go?

A Gift from Burglars

Landing in Khartoum, I was used to the heat after recently being in Nigeria. This was dry heat but still very hot. The airport was a much smaller than the one at which I had first arrived in Lagos. The baggage area did remind me of my first landing in Nigeria — chaos — but this chaos seemed friendlier.

I started to chat to an English man who was waiting near the one and only carousel. He told me he had been in Sudan for many years and was waiting for water pump motors for air coolers. He had not been on the flight but was still in the baggage area; I did not ask how he got there but was more interested in air coolers. He explained that in the dry heat of Khartoum these were as good as air conditioners. The motor pulled air through wet straw and the evaporation caused cooling, the air was more humid and more refreshing than the dry air. Most of the problems came with power cuts and burnt out water pump and fan motors. I asked what happened in the rainy season, thinking of Nigeria. He laughed and said it might rain a couple of times in the year in July or August or even early September. You might see the occasional cloud in the sky but most of the year Khartoum had a bright blue sky with a burning sun.

Finally, the carousel started moving and one bag came out and then, after what seemed a long delay, more bags came out piled on top of each other. My acquaintance chuckled and said to watch the pile up of bags near the end of the carousel, that when the pile became too large, they would stop the carousel. Sure enough, I spied my bag under a mound of other bags. I had to wait while the baggage handlers dismantled the pile. I was holding my duty-free bag and my friend informed me I should have bought it here in the airport — much cheaper than Heathrow. That was something I kept in mind for the future.

Customs and immigration were no problem and I was soon out into the night air. As I was leaving, I noticed a man with a large piece of cardboard with what looked like my name, the letters were a bit distorted but it was my name. He smiled and grabbed my bag and even wanted to carry my duty-free but Nigeria kicked in and I denied him that. The car I entered was an old Morris Minor and I was ushered into the back seat. I don't remember riding in the back seat of a Morris Minor before; although I had driven several when I was much younger. This one had seen better days but started first time.

Getting out of the car park was entertaining as there seemed to be people and cars everywhere although there was no order here. We set off and, being late at night, there was not much traffic; approaching a bridge we were stopped at a police check point. The driver said something in Arabic and pointed towards me and we were waved on. We crossed the Nile and I realized how dark everything was, the city as I looked back had very few lights. Over the bridge we turned onto a road that ran along the Nile; this way was very quiet. The journey seemed to be taking a long time and I was a little apprehensive when the houses seemed to end. We turned onto a road that had some lorry traffic and then finally off that tarmac road onto a dirt one. There were a few houses and then we stopped outside a rather large double storey house. The driver said, "We here." In the darkness the headlights picked out a very large metal gate. There were no lights in the house nor in the adjoining houses, but the moon was almost full, so the area was not pitch black. The driver unlocked the gates and gave me a set of keys; he showed me the gate key and the front door key and put my bag inside the door. Before he left, he told me I would be picked up at seven in the morning. I think that was what he said.

Entering the house, I groped around for a light switch which I finally found. I was in a large room with four 'arm chairs' made from packing case wood, a table and four wicker chairs; the rest of the room was bare. This was the crudest furniture I had ever seen. The light was not too bright, but I found my way to the bedroom where there was a double bed with a thin mattress, some sheets and two pillows. Further examination revealed that under the mattress was a rope bed. I tried it and it did not collapse so I assumed it would be OK. I then found the switch for the air cooler and that started up, blowing fine sand everywhere, but after a short time seemed to work alright. I was by now very tired and collapsed on the bed and slept a good sleep.

I awoke to some muffled noises that seemed to be coming from the floor above. I had noticed that this was a two-storey house, so I assumed someone lived upstairs. It was about six thirty and I needed a shower and had not even opened my suitcase. There were shutters on the window and when I opened them the sun was blinding; what I wanted was a drink. I found the kitchen and in the cupboards were a few glasses and plates, they looked clean so I took a glass. I had read that Khartoum water was good to drink although I had no choice but to pour myself a glass and try. It tasted good and was so refreshing, I had a second glass. The shower was very refreshing too and in the dry heat you almost did not need a towel which I finally found in one of the cupboards.

This was seven a.m. and the heat, was almost unbearable except in the bedroom with the air cooler working. What should I wear? I decided on a shirt, slacks and sandals; this weather was too hot for socks and shoes. I stepped outside to be greeted by a well-dressed Sudanese who wished me good morning in very well-spoken English with a slight accent. This can't be my driver was my first thought.

"I am your neighbour upstairs, my name is Abdul, we heard you come last night and want to welcome you to the vice president's house."

"The vice president of the university?"

"No, the vice president of Sudan."

My initial thoughts were that he should have better furniture than I have in my living room. Abdul then informed me that the driver was waiting outside the gate but there was no rush; there were few times in Sudan when you needed to hurry. This turned out to be very true. I had learned to take things easy in Nigeria, but in Sudan I learned to take things much easier. Abdul invited me to dinner in the evening, but all I could think about was breakfast. He also offered me a lift in the morning if I had to go to the main campus in Khartoum. I explained I had no idea what I would be doing in the next few days but thanked him anyway. "By the way, where are we?" I asked.

"This is called Omdurman Thowra, it is the Omdurman Extension, Khartoum is across the river. By the way, I should switch off the air cooler before you leave otherwise it might not work when you come back"

I said goodbye, switched off the air cooler, locked my door and went outside the gate to the waiting driver. This was the same Morris Minor and the same driver, and I went straight to the back seat. As we motored down the dirt road, I realized in my rush I had forgotten my money and passport, but maybe Abdul was right, no rush. I had no idea where I was going but the ride turned out to be short. We turned into a compound and I recognized the University of Khartoum emblem. This was the Faculty of Education where I would do most of my lecturing. I was introduced to the dean who was a balding middle-aged man with an infectious smile and laugh. He explained we would go to breakfast (fatur) and I would meet some of the other lecturers. Breakfast was a word I wanted to hear as I had not eaten since the plane and Sudan Airways food was not much and not good. I was introduced to several people and their names I quickly forgot, except that there seemed to be several Mohameds and a few Alis. They brought me my breakfast in a shallow bowl; broad beans with onions, a bit of boiled egg and a few herbs on top. I tasted cumin in it too. There was also a large piece of flat bread which looked like wholemeal bread, but I did not think it was made from wheat. I was provided with a spoon but, watching the others, I could see they did not use the spoon but tore off the bread and scooped up the beans. I followed suit and there were a few comments and laughs but I took no notice as the food was good. It was very spicy, but Nigeria had tuned my palate to hot food and these beans were delicious. I found out later that I had been eating with my left hand, which was taboo in Sudan, but I was excused being hawaja (a foreigner). I was hungry and I really enjoyed my breakfast washed down with several glasses of water. Then came the tea poured into small glasses with the teapot well above the glasses giving a dramatic effect. I picked up my glass and was offered sugar, so I took a small teaspoonful; this again seemed to cause amusement at the table. Then to my surprise my companions ladled so much sugar into the glasses that the sugar could not all dissolve; they had saturated solutions. I noticed there were no women at breakfast and commented on my observation to the dean. He smiled and explained that the ladies preferred to eat separately. This was different to Nigeria!

The dean showed me around the campus and I quickly noted that the lecture theatres were more like classrooms and had fans but no air coolers; the only air cooler I saw was in the dean's office. The dean gave me a copy of the curriculum but suggested I would not be needed for about a week and that I should first go to the main campus to sign my contract, get on the payroll and open a bank account. The driver would take me wherever I wanted to go and would be available for a few days.

This time my journey into Khartoum was in daylight and, after picking up my money and passport, I noticed some of the sights along the road. As we entered the main road there was a lot of lorry traffic and the occasional bus, there were also covered vehicles carrying people. I was later to learn these were called boxes or boxy. As with many colloquial words the pronunciation could vary. We detoured off the main road to the road that ran along the Nile. This was an interesting route as we passed boat builders and fishermen, worth a closer look in the future. We approached the bridge and had to join the main road traffic. Luckily there was a policeman directing traffic and he allowed us to get in lane.

As we crossed the bridge this was my first sight of Khartoum and along the Nile road the traffic moved steadily. The driver pointed out the president's palace as we passed the building. That was the only time he had spoken on the journey. His English was quite good, and I was used to English being spoken with a strong accent. We entered the university campus and drove straight to the administration building. This was part of the old Gordon College and it was showing its age. The room I entered needed a good paint job and the only decoration on the wall were two portraits, one of Nimeiry, the president and the other I presumed to be the vice chancellor. The furniture had seen better days and the armchair I was offered was a bit uncomfortable. I was told that this was the office of the registrar and that he would see me as soon as he was free. I was offered tea and a glass of water; both were very welcome as I had not noticed how dry my throat had become. I sat and looked around but there was nothing much of interest except a fan dangling from the high ceiling that was turning very slowly and it seemed to me that it could stop at any time, it looked so exhausted. I drank my tea and water and after a few minutes a short man came into the office. He was dressed in a flowing white robe which I later learned was a jalobia. He introduced himself as the registrar and ushered me into his office. He offered me more tea which I accepted and then he informed me of my duties and gave me a couple of documents to sign. He asked for my passport and assured me I would get it back when the visa had been upgraded so that I could work for the university. I thought that a bit strange as my visa in London had been given to me as a work visa, but he was the registrar and would know the procedure.

Next stop was the bank where I realized I did not have my passport as identification, but my English driving licence and a letter from the registrar seemed sufficient to open an account. I deposited a small amount of money and changed some Sterling for Sudanese pounds. I was now getting hungry and my driver escorted me across the main road to the staff club. I asked if he wanted lunch, but he declined saying he was not allowed in the club and he could get some food elsewhere. He seemed amused that I had offered him lunch. Of course, I had not been aware that the club was only for academic staff. As I wandered in, I noticed all the tables and chairs were in the garden, some under trees or large umbrellas. I stopped at a table and asked the people sitting at it what I should do; they all greeted me with smiles and asked me to join them. I was introduced to the menu and one fellow told me the fried kidneys were good. They called over a waiter and ordered for me, and they apologised for not having any beer in the club. Most of them had spent time in England and they had enjoyed going to the pub. One of them told me his family would not have alcohol in the house, so he had to go to one of the clubs, he was a member of the Syrian club. They also told me there was a British club although none of them had been there. The food came and it was spicy and delicious and of course there was a small glass of tea. I took one sip and realized it was sickly sweet. I asked if I could have just tea, no sugar. This caused lots of laughter and I was told that the Sudanese wasted very little, the exception being sugar in tea. I asked how I should pay but they said they would and would not take no for an answer.

I bade them farewell and found the driver outside the gate; I had been much longer than the thirty minutes we had agreed. I asked him where I could buy beer, which seemed to amuse him but he said he knew a place. I later found out there were many places in the centre of Khartoum but only a few in Omdurman or North Khartoum. As I approached the beer store, I found the man behind the counter was whiter than me. He and I might have been equally white without my suntan. We had a little chat and I found out he was Syrian Druze and had lived in Khartoum for many years but did not go out in the sun. He advised me that the local beer was good, but you could only buy it if you had empty bottles; he only sold cans of imported beer. It was not cheap, but I had developed a thirst for a cold beer. He advised me not to drink on the street as that could cause a problem even for a hawaja. I asked the driver to take me home, but the beer was warming up and the traffic was very slow.

That morning I had been in the kitchen which was quite large, but I had not noticed a fridge, in fact I had not even noticed a stove. My preoccupation had been to get water to drink and I had not explored any of my flat. When I arrived back at my new home, I found there was a fridge, but it had not been switched on and there was a gas stove but no gas. I turned on the fridge and while my beer was cooling in the warm fridge, I found the flat had two bedrooms and at the back a sort of sunroom. The floor was a nice terrazzo floor, but the walls looked like old broken bricks and cement had oozed out onto the floor. The whole interior was a mess and I thought that maybe the builder might be in jail for doing such a shoddy job of the vice president's house.

I wanted to relax but found I was very fidgety; I put it down to jet lag. The whole place was not comfortable — it was too bare. Everywhere I went there was a layer of fine sand covering the furniture and the floor. It even seemed to be in the fridge. The only good feeling was bare feet on the cool terrazzo floor. I unpacked my case and there was a sort of wardrobe but no hangers. I decided I would have to find a better place to live, especially as my wife was going to be joining me in Khartoum soon.

I had been invited to dinner at six p.m. upstairs. After my conversation in the Staff Club I had decided not to take any beer to dinner. I had nothing else except my duty-free which I felt I could not spare. As I was about to leave the power was cut but luckily it was still light. It gets dark very quickly in Sudan. I was ushered onto the roof by my colleague's wife after the round of greetings. I had quickly learned that greetings could go on for a while, but this lady had lived in England and knew how to cut them short. On the roof there was a table and chairs and an old kerosene lamp. I greeted the host and apologised for coming empty handed as I had only beer to bring with me. I was told that his wife did not allow alcohol in the house; I had got it right. This was the first time I had a view of the surroundings; the Nile was about five hundred yards away and in between was a village. My friend informed me that these mud huts were occupied by squatters and the army would come one day and remove them. To the left near the Nile was a brick works and an interesting sight was a donkey cart with what looked like a horizontal barrel on it. My friend informed me that it was a water cart as there was no running water in the village, he also pointed out two large pits where I should not go as these were the latrines. I think he said this area was the 'bara' a word I often used without any Sudanese misunderstanding.

My host's wife bought up the tea and explained that she had put milk in the pot but if I wanted it without milk, she could get me a cup. I thanked her and said this was my first tea with milk in Sudan and then it was poured into a cup not a glass. She asked if I would like sugar and I took a small teaspoonful; as soon as I took a sip of the tea, I realized that it was condensed milk and the tea was so sweet it made the back of my throat tickle. I asked for a glass of water explaining that I always had one when I drank tea. The dinner was fried chicken and chips which I really appreciated. They explained the only time they had 'English' food was at home; if they went out to relatives' or friends' houses they could only get Sudanese food.

By the end of the meal the sun had gone down and it was quite dark, cooling off with a light breeze. The kerosene lamp was useful and, as I left, they loaned me a torch and said I could buy one down at the market. These power cuts were quite frequent and they would often sleep on the roof. Sleeping on the roof was new to me; in Nigeria I would have been afraid of the mosquitoes and the rain.

In the next few weeks, I gave a few lectures, learned some basic Arabic, was able to ride the boxy and found the Sudan Club. The Sudan Club was within walking distance of the main campus of the uni and the restaurant served fish and chips, and roast beef and Yorkshire pudding and had the local beer, Camel. Although the club had a swimming pool another important attraction was that it had a full-size snooker table. I quickly joined a group of players and acquired my own snooker cue, a two-piece metal one. The owner of the cue was leaving and was selling various items including a cue and a car. I approached the finance office of the uni and was able to get a loan for the car. I did not want to use money from the UK and found the interest loan on the car was much lower than I could have obtained in the UK. The only stipulation was that I had to get it tested at the government vehicle station. The car was a Hillman, a few years old but it seemed in perfect working order; it even had an air conditioner. I later found that the air conditioner could not cope well with Khartoum heat and traffic.

One Saturday morning I drove to the testing station to find that eight thirty a.m. was breakfast 'fatur' time. There were several cars waiting to be tested in front of mine, so I decided to wander over to where the mechanics were having breakfast. I was invited to come and join them, which I did. There was a large communal plate of beans, similar to what I was used to at the Faculty of Education, and they all dipped their bread into the one plate. I was offered bread and I remembered to use my right hand to get the beans. It was spicy, they had used a good dose of red pepper, but it tasted good. I had two dips into the plate and they were very pleased. Consequently, my car was the first one to be tested and of course it passed. The mechanics all shook my hand and invited me back any day for breakfast.

Now I had a car the only problem was petrol; it was always in short supply and rationed. I could not go to Khartoum every day and I often had to queue for hours for petrol — one time I queued overnight. That meant I had to ride the boxy to Omdurman and then try to get transport to Khartoum. The main centre for transport was Omdurman souk (the market) which was a good place to shop but not to catch a bus. One day each week I had a two-hour lecture from ten to twelve in the Faculty of Education and then another two-hour lecture from four to six p.m. on the main campus. That meant getting to Omdurman after midday when I suspected most of the transport drivers took a siesta. It was a fight to get on one of the too scarce buses and one time I rode on the back of a truck, much to the amusement of the other passengers. Getting home at night was often easier and not so hot but still took time. I realized that I could not bring my wife to Thowra, and so I applied to the housing department for somewhere in Khartoum. My journeys from Omdurman to Khartoum and back were always interesting though, many times I was not allowed to pay my fare.

While I was awaiting my new lodgings, I had some unwelcome visitors. It was at about one a.m. and there was a power cut. I was only half asleep and I heard a couple of bangs. My first thought was that I must have left a door open and the wind was the cause of the noise. Then I heard a louder bang and decided to get up to investigate. As I entered the living room in my underpants and bare feet, I looked down the hallway towards the sunroom. In the moonlight I saw two shiny heads coming through the door. I put my hands to my face and gave out a loud roar that echoed in the bare concrete-walled room. Two shiny heads did an about face and ran for the door. I was about to chase them when I thought I should arm myself. I found the butt end of my snooker cue and chased down the hallway. Of course, they were gone but they left me a gift: a bent screwdriver they had used to prise open the door. I did not expect them back as they probably believed I had a lion in my house.

The Left-Handed Sudanese

Early one Saturday morning, I was on my way to work and stopped off at the Sudan Club to talk to the manager. I was the secretary of the club and I wanted to make sure there had not been a problem on Friday night with unruly members. Friday night always seemed to be the time for some drunken member or members to cause a problem. Most of the newer expatriates were not used to Friday being a holiday and Saturday or even Sunday being a working day. I was informed that the manager was out checking the new law. I did not think much of it and proceeded to work on the outskirts of Omdurman. During my drive I mulled over the possible new law, employment or advertising or almost anything. Whatever the new law it was probably going to be a problem for us. The manager, a Coptic Christian was our link to the varying regulations, which were always changing. He was young and energetic and got on well with most of the members, but he could not be bullied. He could be very firm when the rules were ignored.

The Sudan Club was the British club, a hangover from colonial times. It was set up when Sudan became independent, and the new Sudanese government dictated the rules for membership. Before independence there had been three British clubs; one for Diplomats, and high-ranking civil servants and military officers. The second was for other civil servants and military officers and the third club was for non-commissioned officers NCOs and ordinary soldiers. These were to be merged into one club and the stipulation for membership was that members must be holders of a British passport. A few years later the rules were relaxed so that 10% of the membership could be Commonwealth citizens. These rules were enshrined in the constitution and fully supported by the new Sudanese government. The merging of all classes into one club may have been a Muslim ethos that all men are equal but in 1950s Britain this was not what would have been done at home.

The Sudanese government probably wanted to keep an eye on their previous rulers, and the members assumed that some of the staff were paid informants of the government. The staff, particularly the cooking staff, had been well trained by the colonial masters and they knew how to cook steak and kidney pie, bangers and mash and a good Yorkshire pudding. The Sudanese members who were married to Brits liked the anachronism of the rules and they could invite friends and relatives to this exclusive club. The members could have tried to change the rules but there was no enthusiasm for such an act; no one wanted to rock the boat.

Later in the afternoon I returned from work to the club, entered through the gates and was confronted by a member.

"Why are the bars closed?"

"Are they?"

"Yes, they have been shut since three o'clock by orders of the president."

"Well if the president ordered them shut there must have been a good reason."

A typical member wants the club to run smoothly, but if anyone takes a decision he does not like, he is up in arms. I assumed the president, Roger, had good reason for closing the bar but even I could have welcomed a cold beer. Lately we had had a problem with the beer — the bottles were exploding. The local beer, 'Camel', had taken on a lethal streak. The brewery had run out of the chemical used to kill the yeast and the beer was live. The bar staff would gingerly reach into the fridge and take out a beer, then they would wrap a cloth round the beer before opening it. The process was a source of amusement with the members, but they all seemed to like the new beer.

The club was open, but the office was closed and so I had to find the head barman. Ali spoke good English, he had been a barman in the top British club, and as I approached him, he had a grin on his face.

"Ali, what has happened?"

"It is Sharia law, sir, God's law. No drinking."

"Where is the manager?"

"He is talking to the government."

"What happens now?"

"I do not know, sir, but we must shut the bar and not sell alcohol, but we can sell food."

Now I was really confused and I tried remembering about Sharia law. I knew it was applied in Saudi Arabia and all I could think of was some of the more gruesome aspects. It could not apply to us as we were Christians, and this was a private club. As I drove to Roger's house, I thought it must be a mistake, but he was not reassuring.

Roger said, "All the beer and liquor stores have been closed and they are emptying them. The rumour goes that they are going to throw all the booze into the Nile." I laughed at the thought of all that beer and liquor being dumped in the Nile; it seemed hilarious to me.

"I have locked the beer store just in case we get raided by the police and I have the keys. The bar stock has been moved to the barman's store and the staff have been ordered to serve no more beer whatever threats the members make. I think we should meet tomorrow at lunch time and assess the situation." Roger was in a much more sober mood than I; this was now starting to seem like a real problem.

After a few cold beers, I left Roger's place and drove to my apartment. My drive took me past several of the beer stores and they were all closed except one which was being emptied by the army. The police were controlling the crowd that had gathered and they waved me on in a manner that indicated I should get out of there. I started to think about my situation. I had bought a case of beer the previous Thursday, but friends had been over to play darts on the Friday. I probably had less than a dozen beers and now I was cursing myself for not buying more. No one would sell me a case now!

Life in a developing country is like that: buy twice as much as you need, because when you run out there will be none available. I was displaying the basic feeling of the insecurity of the expat, but this was serious, it was my beer! Khartoum can be very hot and, although I had acclimatized to some degree, you had to drink plenty of fluids. The one fluid I liked was beer, but a cold glass of Khartoum water came a close second. I remember driving to the club from Omdurman and consuming a whole jug of cold water before my first beer with a meal. September was nearly always a hot month and the temperature never started to fall till late November. I consoled myself with the belief that this Sharia would not last long and surely the law would not apply to the expats, otherwise most of the expats would leave.

I arrived home and immediately went to the fridge; eleven cans of beer, two bottles of lemon wine and one bottle of watermelon wine was the sum total of my alcoholic drinks. I took a can and started to guzzle the contents when I stopped and thought I should make it last. The only problem is that with a room temperature of nearly forty degrees the beer soon becomes warm and I don't like ice in my beer.

The next day I went to work and came back to the club for lunch at about one o'clock and was met at the gate by the manager, Kamal. "We have a problem," said the manager.

"Yes, it is called Sharia."

"This is immediate. There are two men in my office and they have come to take the stock. One is a policeman and the other is a military police officer." I was at a loss for words except a few profane ones, but I would have to be diplomatic.

As I entered the office, I said, "We have sent for the president." Actually, Kamal had already told them that, but I thought they might believe it from me. I was now introduced to the officers and I realized my gaff: I should have greeted them first before getting down to business. But that was not my first and would not be my last indiscretion in dealing with Sudanese.

My greeting to the 'red cap' military officer was met with a steely stare and a slight nod; I decided that this Sudanese was not so friendly. My greeting to the policeman was met with a smile and I noticed he had a pen in his left hand. I asked if he was left-handed and he said he was. I immediately warmed to him as I am left-handed and during my time in Africa, I had observed very few left handers. In Nigeria none of my educated friends was left-handed, and in Sudan I had not come across a left-handed Sudanese student with one exception. One student with a Sudanese father and a Bulgarian mother was left-handed. She told me that her early years in school had been in Bulgaria, and she was allowed to write with her left hand. I remarked to the policeman that I had a similar 'problem' and scribbled something on a paper. He was obviously pleased and started to tell me about his family.

His father was left-handed and so was one of his brothers. The father had had limited schooling and more or less taught himself to write, but he had had a tough time when he did attend school. His family, friends and teachers had all cajoled or encouraged him to write with his right hand, but he was stubborn. They all looked on him as being strange and obstinate for wanting to do something other than clean himself with his left hand. Of course, he had to eat with his right hand; eating with his left hand would have been a totally antisocial act not tolerated in his society. When he became proficient at writing, people in the village would marvel at his ability. When he came to Khartoum, he found a few other left handers, but they were all white men. He had seven children and two of them were left-handed, the policeman being one of them. I interrupted. "Same mother?"

"Yes," replied the policeman.

The army officer was getting restless, so I ordered some tea, the Sudanese way. I apologised for the delay but explained that the president had the keys, failing to mention there was a spare set in the safe. The policeman and I carried on our conversation, and he did not seem at all impatient. He explained how his brother had had a tough time particularly at junior school. His father had gone to the school and demonstrated how a left hander could write as well if not better than a right hander, and that satisfied most of the teachers. The policeman's brother had paved the way in junior school, and in senior school he had gone to a Catholic school where his teacher was left-handed.

Their father was a trader and wanted his sons to have the best education available in Khartoum and, although a Muslim, had sent them to the Catholic school run by Italian priests. Although the teachers were Italian the education was in English and Arabic. Their father was so pleased he donated a sum of money to the school so that other Sudanese children could get a scholarship.

The red cap was losing patience and so I entertained them by showing how some American and Canadian left handers would imitate right handers. They would hook their hand above the pen so they could drag the pen across the page like a right-handed person. This even seemed to amuse the army officer.

I was getting a bit stressed by the time the tea finally arrived. The tea came in small glasses with no milk and I watched with amusement both Sudanese put four teaspoons of sugar in a small glass of tea. We were sipping tea when Roger arrived, to my relief.

Introductions were made and the red cap intimated he was in a hurry to view and count the stock. Roger and I were in much less of a hurry, but we could have no objections. As we walked to the store, I briefed Roger on the disposition of the two men. Roger's comment was that the red cap probably wanted to take the stock to the barracks to supply the army.

Our store was fully stocked; we had recently bought two thousand cases of beer and were planning to buy more before Christmas. The store was cooled by two large air coolers and on this hot dry day they were doing an excellent job. Entering the store was a pleasant experience, the only problem was the mental image of all that booze being destroyed. Roger and I were probably thinking similar thoughts, if only we could smuggle a few cases to our homes we would be happy. The manager was hinting that they could reduce the numbers on their list, but they were having none of it. They were taking no nonsense and they wanted all the bar stock and anything in the 'closed rooms' (such as more bar stock) to be removed to the store, even the empty bottles. The final, killer blow was that they were going to seal the store and bring a truck the next day to empty the store. This news had Roger and I thinking, but not voicing, evil thoughts.

The policeman presented a stock list which we had to sign, and we were each given a copy. They left and we, the manager, Roger and I, went into a huddle. Time was too short. What could we do to avert the looming disaster? Our thoughts and conversation were broken by a member demanding a beer for his lunch. In a way it was light relief to explain Sharia law to him and how it would affect his life: he was obviously not pleased. It was decided to go through diplomatic channels; maybe we could get to a chief of police or the head of the army. One Sudanese member came up and, eavesdropping on our conversation, suggested that the only way was to go to the top, President Numeri. That was a good suggestion but there was no hope of it happening. The lunch definitely lacked a couple of beers to wash it down.

The British ambassador was at home on Sunday afternoon and was very helpful. The ambassador was the patron of the club but none of the ambassadors had interfered or even had much to do with the club. Most expats have a poor opinion of their embassies, thinking them unresponsive, but this was not the case this time. The ambassador promised all the help he could and even phoned the undersecretary in the Ministry of Foreign Affairs while we were enjoying his hospitality: a cold beer. We discussed who we were to approach to stop the emptying of our store, tomorrow! The ambassador suggested that the police might be more receptive than the army, the police chief would be a better bet than an army general who may have no control over the red caps.

As we left the ambassador's residence, we were all smiles and hopeful we could stop this waste of good booze that kept our expatriates happy. Kamal was very impressed with the ambassador's residence, particularly the cold room which was as big as any apartment in Khartoum. Kamal had declined a beer, taking a lemonade, and he had wandered around the gardens as we were discussing our problem. As we left the residence Kamal was enthralled with the house but Roger and I were full of hope. Could we avert the dumping of our booze in the Nile?

Our drive to the police headquarters was more pleasurable in the knowledge that we could put a brake on a very drastic action. It was about five p.m. when we arrived. As we entered, there was a big crowd, many of whom seemed to know our manager. "Kamal, who are these people?" Roger asked.

"They are all beer store owners and they are here demanding compensation."

I had not thought about compensation; we could think about carrying out some repairs and alterations, but that would be futile without booze to bring in the members. Roger, ever the accountant, may have had similar thoughts, but he said, "Compensation is no good to us. Today's takings are probably about a quarter of last Sunday's takings."

We were ushered into an outer office after we had introduced ourselves, leaving the crowd outside. The police chief was expected shortly and we were offered chairs (which were not too comfortable) and tea. The office was bare and the tea sweet. The building was an old colonial-style building with high ceilings and thick brick walls. The paint was old and peeling and a lone fan dangling from the ceiling creaked as it slowly turned. The electrics were an unbelievable mess; there seemed to be wires running everywhere. The fuse box was open and there were wires coming out of it running in every direction to light and wall sockets. The original wiring in the walls was defunct, probably due to overloading, and someone had ordered a quick repair job.

The police chief arrived and by his smile we thought him to be possibly sympathetic to our plight. He was not in uniform but was wearing a jalobia, which to me was a good sign. We explained our problem and, although he was sympathetic, he was noncommittal. He pointed out that the crowd outside had the same problems, but he had no immediate answers. We told him that diplomatic wheels were in motion and we were hoping that he could delay any actions that would remove our stock. Kamal gave the name of the left-handed policeman who, fortunately, was stationed there at the headquarters. The police chief said the officer would be warned to wait for more instructions. The junior officer taking notes was told to see that this instruction was passed on. The chief offered us more tea, but we declined and left; he was going to have a busy evening.

When we returned to the club it was almost deserted and the few members present had lots of questions. The mood was anxious but there was a calming effect when we told them the ambassador was involved. "It will never last, this Sharia." These words were spoken by one of the older members, but Sharia has lasted in the Sudan and most of the expats have not left.

Much of the beer, wine and liquor from the beer stores was taken to the Nile, where steam rollers crushed the bottles and cans then pushed the debris into the Nile. The joke was that there were probably a lot of drunken crocodiles.

The last information I had was that the stock was still locked in the store. The air coolers had been switched off and with an average room temperature of forty degrees the beer would be undrinkable, but the liquor could still be good and the wine might be interesting.

I did see the left-handed policeman one more time. He came about a week after our first meeting to check that the lock seals were not broken. I assured him that the British club would never break the law.

Juba

Alan was lecturing in science at Khartoum University. He had been recruited in the UK as a lecturer and a tax-free salary in the UK had been offered as an inducement. Alan had received offers from industries in the UK, but this overall salary package was better. Arriving in Khartoum just after Sharia had been declared, had been a bit of a shock. Alan was not an excessive drinker but he was used to a few pints down the pub. He was met at the airport by an English colleague who lamented the fact that before the new law was introduced Alan could have bought half a gallon of whisky at a good price at the duty-free shop.

Alan was prepared for the desert and the heat; at least he thought he was. This dry heat meant he was never sweating but was continually thirsty. He learned to drink lots of water and fruit juice. He disliked the soft, fizzy drinks; they were too sweet and too much fruit juice did not agree with him. The best fruit juice was at the Sudan Club but he did learn to make his own. He confided in Abdu, one of his Sudanese colleagues, that he missed a cold beer. The lecturer admitted that while studying in the UK he was a regular visitor to the pub, but he was now married to a devout Muslim woman who was vehemently against alcohol. Sharia had stopped his beer consumption, but he had relatives in Egypt who he visited regularly. Egyptian beer was good and many of them similar to German beers. Abdu confided that many of his friends often visited Egypt or Ethiopia for refreshments.

Abdu invited Alan to a barbecue where they would have goat and lamb and other Sudanese dishes, but unfortunately no alcohol. Alan asked if he could bring anything but was told the host provided everything. His friend said there would be a few relatives and friends but most of them spoke decent English, but he would be the only non-Sudanese present although he might not be the whitest man there; they would all be men. At that remark, Alan had been about to ask a question but was cut short by Abdu saying his cousin, a taxi driver, would pick him up — a free ride in a taxi!

Alan was looking forward to this barbecue which, of course, was to be held on a Friday. The comment about a whiter white man was intriguing him. At five p.m. sharp he was picked up by a cabbie called Mohamed, who was on time, spoke pretty good English and drove carefully; what a delight. Abdu's house was not large but had a decent size garden, it was in an area Alan had not visited called Riad and Alan admitted he may not have found the house left to his own devices. The garden was green and obviously well-watered and there were some pretty flowers around the walls. Alan felt immediately at home; the only decent garden he knew was at the Sudan Club but this was more intimate. Most of the guests were already there and Abdu introduced Alan to about twelve men whose names he immediately forgot. He did notice the 'white' man and sat next to him. It turned out that Isam was Syrian but had lived most of his life in Khartoum and avoided the sun like the plague. Isam had a shop in the souk selling textiles and providing tailoring services. On the other side of Alan was a man called Ali who was one of Abdu's relatives. He was a pilot in the Air Force and had a few stories to tell about aviation in the Sudan. Alan was enjoying the company and, when the food came, which was mainly shish kebabs, he let it slip that it would go down well with a beer. Everyone laughed, and Alan thought he had made a mistake. Isam laughed and agreed, and Ali came out with the most surprising comment.

"I know where you can get a beer: Juba. I don't drink but as a good Muslim I understand the needs of others."

Alan was taken aback but did not reply until one of Abdu's young relatives said, "Let's go to Juba."

"How are we going to get to Juba?" was Alan's reply.

"Well I am going there in a couple of days and I can take a couple of passengers. It will be an overnight stop unless there is a problem," replied Ali.

Alan thought quickly, "I can get a couple of days off work, but do I need my passport?"

"No passport required, you will be on a military aircraft, but bring some ID as you might be challenged in Juba. There will be accommodation on the military compound but it might be a little rough."

Alan had not seen any of Sudan except Khartoum and now he had the opportunity to see southern Sudan. The young Sudanese who wanted to go was also enthusiastic as he had only seen northern Sudan. Hassan was nearly eighteen and was about to go to university but he had never been outside Khartoum; even Omdurman was unknown to him.

Alan had some contact with the British Council and when he found out they had a compound in Juba, he contacted the head of the council and requested an overnight stay in Juba. This was no problem as the compound was almost empty and they were glad to get feedback about Juba from any independent Brit. Taking a couple of days off work was easy, but the dean had a word of caution, saying, "You know Juba is in a war zone." Actually, Alan had not thought about that and had little knowledge of the problems in the Sudan.

At seven a.m. Alan arrived at the airport and was directed to the military compound gate. Hassan was there waiting impatiently to get in, but the security was very tight and so they had to wait until Ali came and escorted them to the tarmac. Ali explained that he needed to examine the plane and no one would be allowed on before he gave the all-clear. Alan was pleased that it seemed to be an efficient operation. As soon as Ali gave the word, they were ushered onto the plane and into the cockpit. There was a bench seat directly behind the pilot and co-pilot and they were told to sit there and buckle up the safety harness. Ali came aboard and told them this was a Buffalo with four engines and a payload in the back. They were taking off to the south and would basically follow the White Nile to Juba. In the meantime, he introduced the co-pilot and navigator who both spoke excellent English. Alan was overjoyed as he was going to be able to see the runway as they took off and as they landed. Hassan was also excited as this was his first time in a plane. They both sat in silence as the plane took off smoothly and both were smiling for about five minutes when an alarm sounded. Ali nonchalantly told them one of the engines was having a problem but not to worry there were three other engines. That put a bit of a damper on the excitement of the passengers on the bench seat.

Alan was almost totally ignorant of the problems in the south of Sudan and other parts of the country. He was living in a sort of cocoon in Khartoum and, having no TV or understanding of Arabic, he did not know there was a war on. The navigator filled him in on a few of the details, which made Alan realise they were flying into a war zone. The South Sudanese Liberation Army led by a Colonel Garang had their headquarters in Bor on the Nile and they were soon to fly over the town. Alan's heart was definitely beating faster, and when he was told they had anti-aircraft missiles his concentration level went up a notch.

His anxiety went up another notch when the navigator pointed down and said, "I think that is Bor."

"You think that is Bor?" Ali chimed in and said that it was Bor and the rebels did not seem to want a shot at them, but that it could be different when they descended into Juba. Now Alan wanted to turn back. Were a few beers worth this stress? Ali explained they were flying high enough to deter any attempted missile attack.

"What about Juba?" Alan asked.

"Juba is surrounded by hills, or jebels, and we think the rebels may hold one or two of them. Our approach is to fly in high, do a few circles and drop quickly into the airport. Don't worry they have not shot a plane down for a long time." Ali was speaking quite calmly, but Alan was now sweating.

Their approach into Juba was just as Ali had said, and Alan's eyes were glued to the runway as they landed. It was a good landing and at last Alan could look around. Not much of an airport with just one or two old planes around and a Sudanese Airways plane parked at the end of the runway. As they came to a standstill Alan could see a military deputation on the tarmac awaiting their arrival but no band playing. That thought bought a smile to Alan's face and he began to relax. Ali asked that when they reached the tarmac, they move to one side with the navigator, Ali would have some formalities to attend to and the co-pilot would arrange transport for them to go to the Juba Hotel.

As they stood on the tarmac awaiting their transport, the contents started to unload from the back of the plane. There seemed to be about fifty soldiers, each with a rifle, and the navigator explained the rifles were in case of trouble at the airport. What happened next was a bigger shock, they unloaded a cold dewar with a little of the contents spilling and immediately vaporizing. "What is that?"

"It is liquid oxygen for the MIG jets."

"Oh my god, we have been flying with a platoon of soldiers with loaded rifles and a dewar of liquid oxygen spilling out." This is going to be a very welcome beer, thought Alan.

As they entered the Juba Hotel compound, they stopped to let a cyclist come out and on the back of his bike was a huge fish. "What is that fish?" asked Alan.

"That is a Nile perch" replied the navigator. One look at this hotel and Alan was glad he was staying elsewhere. The walls and the doors seemed to be covered in moss or some green stuff. They sat down at a table in the courtyard and ordered a late lunch. Hassan and Alan decided to have Nile perch and the navigator had steak and eggs, the order included two beers and a soft drink for Hassan. "I thought you were a Muslim," asked Alan of the Navigator.

"I am, but I love beer and I volunteered for this flight to refresh my thirst. Tonight, at the dinner in the commander's house, we will drink lots. We will all be invited to dinner and we all drink except the captain who is teetotal. I expect there will be whisky as well as beer."

The Nile perch was delicious; it had been barbecued with a little spice and Alan thought this crumby hotel had a good chef. While they were eating, Ali arrived and said the navigator and Hassan would go to the military compound and at about six p.m. a driver would pick Alan up from the British Council compound. The compound was just across the street from the Juba Hotel so he did not have far to walk. Alan paid the bill and walked out into the street. It was not much of a street as the tarmac edges were all crumbling and there were no road markings. He walked up to the guard at the British Council compound and introduced himself. The guard ushered him into the office where he met the local British Council resident. He was an older man with a northern English accent and said he was pleased to see Alan. He explained that they only had two temporary visitors, an American working for an aid agency and a visiting academic at the university. They had a library open to the locals and two Sudanese kept an eye on that. Books here were so important, they had to watch they did not disappear. Alan had been in the library in Khartoum and they did not have much problem with books disappearing there, but here the shortage of everything put extra value on things such as books. The locals knew that the only way out of this troublesome place was English and education. On a lighter note they had a swimming pool and Alan regretted not bringing swimming trunks.

Alan was shown to his room where he dropped his bag and was offered a ride to see the sites of Juba. Alan climbed into the oldest, most dilapidated Land Rover he had ever seen and was surprised the car started first go. The resident told him they had a better car, but it was only for official occasions. At this time Juba had only about one mile of tarmac road from the airport to near the university. Juba University was open and working; the students had not taken the lead from the students in Khartoum and were still hard at work. In Khartoum some students had held a demonstration and the university had been closed for a couple of days. There seemed to be lots of police around the campus, so they did not enter. The market was almost deserted as it was late afternoon. There were very few houses with more than two stories but lots of roadside bars. Juba was a quiet little town with nothing much to see. They headed for the river where there were some old abandoned barges and a few small craft. The resident, Jim, explained that there would normally be lots of river traffic but the rebels were holding a section of the river and only letting a few boats through. The only way to get goods in was by road from Kenya, Uganda or the Republic of the Congo. Jim explained that there were many problems on all the routes with lots of road blocks. Most of the Arab traders who ran the truck traffic were probably playing bribes to get through to

Juba. In twenty minutes, that was Juba visited. Jim explained that the rebels were close and probably had lots of informers in Juba, but they had not bothered expats. The local tribe was in a difficult position, as if they openly supported the rebels, they would be arrested but if they supported the government they could be killed if the rebels took over.

Back in his room, Alan showered and put on a clean shirt. He wondered how formal this dinner would be but he had very few clothes to choose from. The guard knocked on his door to say that a military vehicle was waiting at the gate. A short ride to the garrison compound was over quickly and Alan was not sure what he expected. There was nothing special except a two-story house and a series of buildings that looked like stables, probably for the troops. On entering the main building Alan was introduced to the commandant and a couple of his officers. Alan noted several ladies who were not dressed like the Muslim women in Khartoum. Hassan quickly pulled Alan aside and quietly asked if he could stay with Alan that night. Alan said, "I suppose so, but why?"

"They have set me up with one of these women and I am scared."

"Who has set you up?"

"The crew, they are all going to get drunk and sleep with these women."

Alan could see the problem and he quickly thought of the villa in which he was staying. He thought it had a second bed but had not taken too much notice. "You might have to sleep on the floor."

"I'll sleep anywhere but not here."

They were standing in a large room and when the double doors were opened to reveal a table full of food, the ladies were quick off the mark. The commandant smiled and said, "They are hungry." Alan was ushered to the front of the queue and put a small amount on his plate. When the co-pilot whispered there would be no seconds, Alan added a little more. The food was good and tasty, and he said so to the commandant.

"The chef is a southerner who worked for the British governor before independence," answered the commandant. After a couple of beers and a whisky Alan approached Ali and asked if it would be impolite to leave so early; he also informed Ali that he was taking Hassan with him for 'protection'. Ali laughed and said he understood and told Alan and Hassan that he would send for the driver while they thanked the commandant.

Hassan was so relieved when they got into the jeep and left the military compound. Hassan had only drunk one beer and hoped his mother would not find out. Alan was laughing inside with the thought of Hassan sleeping with one of those 'ladies'. The streets were deserted but around each roadside bar there was a crowd having a good time — no Sharia in this part of the south.

The room in the British Council compound did have two beds so Hassan did not have to sleep on the floor. Next morning, they had a simple breakfast in the compound and awaited their transport. Alan wanted to pay for the breakfast but was told to keep his money. The resident was interested in the party the night before and said he would change it a bit and get it into his monthly report.

As they approached the airport, they could see troops lined up to be loaded on to the Buffalo. They all had rifles which Alan hoped were not loaded. While they were waiting on the tarmac they were approached by a white man. He introduced himself as a BBC correspondent and asked if they were going back to Khartoum. The man had been stuck in Juba since the Sudan Airways flights had been cancelled and was desperate to get back to Khartoum. Alan explained that the only person who could help was the pilot, Ali, and pointed him out. After talking to Ali, the BBC correspondent came back and was pleased to announce he could sit in the rear with the troops.

Alan was a bit apprehensive about the take-off and was continually scanning the hills around Juba. The co-pilot and navigator both had severe hangovers and Ali, the captain and non-drinker, had a migraine headache. At one stage Ali asked the co-pilot if he would take over, but he declined and Ali with a migraine had to do all the work. Alan was sweating thinking that this was not going well and they had not yet left Juba.

Hassan was so glad Alan had sheltered him from a potential stay in the military compound with all the predatory people. As they were approaching Khartoum, the navigator got word that there was a sandstorm (haboob) in Khartoum and that they may not be able to land. That woke everybody up, and Ali said they had to land as one of the engines was playing up. "Don't worry this plane can fly on two engines and I know Khartoum Airport very well," he said. Everyone in the cockpit was now very alert and as they got closer to Khartoum it appeared that the haboob had lessened and the lights on the runway were switched on.

Coming in to land everyone's eyes were on the runway; it was pretty clear as the haboob had gone on its way. There appeared to be some sand blowing across the runway, but that was pretty normal for Khartoum. As the plane came to rest, a deputation came from the terminal to greet the returning soldiers and airmen. There was an audible sigh of relief as the plane came to a stop. Alan and Hassan descended from the cockpit and stood to one side. As the soldiers came from the back of the plane, the BBC man approached Alan. "That was a very smooth flight, thank you for getting me on it. I found a few soldiers with some English and we had a good discussion about Juba." Alan smiled weakly as he was still a bit shaken by the flight, but he said nothing to the journalist.

Back in his flat he found a bottle of Aragi, (a sprit made from dates), and had a good drink. This was two days he would not forget. In the morning despite a good night's sleep he woke with pains in his stomach. He wondered whether it was appendicitis. He drove to

Abdu's uncle's hospital and found Hassan there with the same symptoms. The doctor examined them both, discounted appendicitis. and asked what they had eaten the previous day. They had both eaten the Nile perch and the doctor laughed. "The fishermen often catch that fish with poison bate, and I think that is the source of your pain. Take these pain killers and go to bed — you may have to use the toilet regularly."

Khartoum Trilogy
Aid to Africa

Kathy hadn't intended to become an aid worker in Africa. She had graduated in social science from the University of Aston in Birmingham. Her graduation had coincided with a down-turn in the job market, so she had had to take a job in a department store. In many ways the job was boring but she spent much of her time studying people. She would spend her lunch times walking around Birmingham city centre observing shoppers and passers-by. One day she came across an African preacher trying to tell the passing shoppers about the error of their ways. She was intrigued by this elderly man and started to talk to him. He said he was bringing Christianity back from Africa, to this land that he had always thought to be religious. He was shocked by the 'heathen' outlook of the Brits he had met.

Kathy had little interest in religion but the people in Africa intrigued her. She would meet Emmanuel in her lunch hour and after a bit of preaching he would tell her about Africa. He was originally from Ghana but had travelled extensively. He had lived and preached in many countries in West and East Africa. They talked about religions, places, tribalism and corruption.

Emmanuel was quite emotional about how the poor and rich lived and how money was siphoned off into a few pockets. These conversations sparked Kathy's interest in travelling to Africa.

Aston University was quite close to the centre of Birmingham and she would often drop in to see the jobs advertised on the notice boards. One day a job was advertised with an organization specializing in aid to Africa. The advert was almost an anti-advert. The pay was poor, the living standards would be much lower than British standards, the hours were long and the work was hard. There was no 'come on' in this advert but Kathy was sucked in by *Africa*. She applied and discussed the job with Emmanuel; his first question was where in Africa? Kathy suddenly realized there was no information in the advert, so she would have to ask lots of questions in the interview.

After a week she received a reply accepting her for the job as she was the best qualified applicant; later she found out she was the only applicant. There was a number to call if she wanted to accept the job offer; this was the chance to ask questions. The call was fairly short as most of the questions remained unanswered and the only question she really had to know was only partially answered. The aid programme was very fluid, and she could be sent to Chad, Ethiopia, Sudan or the Central African Republic. Despite the uncertainty she still accepted the job. Kathy was not normally impetuous, and she had surprised herself at how quickly she had said yes.

The next time she met Emmanuel, Kathy invited him for a coffee so she could find out about these countries. Emmanuel had not been in Chad but knew it was a very poor country needing lots of aid. Ethiopia was wracked with poor harvests and was in dire need of food aid. He had been there and told her about a very ancient orthodox form of Christianity which meant a woman might find some problems dealing with men. The Central African Republic always seemed to be at war and was not a safe place. Emmanuel knew most about the Sudan. He had lived in Khartoum, the capital, and although dominated by Muslims there were many Christians of various denominations. Khartoum was a trading city and so had attracted a wide variety of people of all nations. In the south there were many Christians and the southern capital Juba was the place he loved best. He had preached in many towns in South Sudan and although a very tribal place he was able to cross tribal boundaries and attract enthusiastic congregations.

Kathy realized that preaching came first with Emmanuel but at least she had some information about where she might be going in Africa. She awaited a telephone call from her future employer and when it came, she was told she would be reimbursed for her travel expense to London and put up in a hotel. She was to bring her passport so as to start the visa processes.

The local library had little information about Sudan. There was some history including General Gordon losing his head and Kitchener's army vanquishing the Mahdi's army. There was some information about the geography but little about current life in the Sudan. Kathy could not wait to fill in the enormous gaps in her knowledge.

Arriving at Euston, she was met by an elderly, smartly dressed man who introduced himself as John. They took a taxi to a block of flats in Kensington which John told her was his home and office. The flat was well furnished with one of the bedrooms used as an office. There were several filing cabinets and a rather large desk and several chairs. John came straight to the point, he was a management consultant but his real passion was his aid company, registered as a charity and supported by donations or sponsorship from companies. He used his consultancy to get funds from donors and did not take a salary from his aid company. The hotel Kathy was to stay in had donated her room for the night. John explained that many companies would donate and could claim the tax relief but did not want any publicity about their donations.

"My consultancy puts food on my plate, but my aid work puts food on many plates."

John had worked and lived in the Sudan in his extensive travels and had decided to help as best he could. One of the Sudanese he worked with was now manager of the Khartoum office. He had a manager in offices in Chad, Ethiopia and the Central African Republic but the main operation was in the Sudan. The main/most important part of the aid was to get food and medical supplies to the refugee camps which were near the borders of Sudan. A sea shipment to Port Sudan was the easiest way of getting the aid into Sudan, but it was a long way to the borders of Chad and the Central African Republic. Some airlines had flights into Chad and if they would freely donate cargo space, he could get some provisions in that way. Supplies to the Central African Republic were much more difficult as there were always some local violent conflicts going on and regular freight flights to that country were very few. He relied on getting donations in Kenya and buying products to send by road to South Sudan.

Kathy was very impressed with John's enthusiasm and loved the maps showing shipping routes and refugee camps. This was filling in much of the detail that had been unavailable from Emmanuel. At last she was able to ask the question that had been continually in her brain.

"Why do you want to hire me?"

"Two major reasons: I need feedback from someone unfamiliar with our operation and someone who can tell our sponsors the successes, failures and difficulties of what we are trying to do. The second is that the right-hand man to the manager in Khartoum has been poached by a bigger aid organization."

"Where will I be based?"

"Initially you will be in Khartoum but later in Juba. From Khartoum you will travel to the Ethiopian border and organize shipments coming from Port Sudan. You may have to go to Port Sudan and follow the shipments to the camps. These convoys often pass through areas close to starvation and attacks are not unknown and there may have to be negotiations with the locals. We do have armed guards on the convoys, but we would like to avoid shooting starving people. Your presence and giving them a small portion of the cargo may help out in tricky situations."

"When will I leave?"

"I expect your visa will take about a week as I have contacts in the Sudanese Embassy and they like what we are doing. I will contact you and hope you can fly out immediately."

"I could fly out today," Kathy replied excitedly.

Arriving back in Birmingham Kathy sought out Emmanuel. She told him about the job and the aid organization and was expecting a positive response, but it was not as enthusiastic as she had expected. The aid programme was good but her role in it could be difficult. She realized she had not asked any questions about living conditions, but she really did not care — she had the job.

"The African male is not used to taking orders from women. In the house she may be queen but outside she may not have much of a voice. A role in which you are going to tell several males what to do could be tricky."

Emmanuel spoke in a very serious tone. "The north of Sudan is mainly Muslim and dealing with men could be more difficult than in South Sudan. You will have to be careful to avoid upsetting religious and cultural ways of doing things."

Kathy was not too happy with the negative side of Emmanuel's advice but she realized she had a lot to learn. After just a week she was informed by John that her passport was ready and her flight booked on Sudan Airways. She was warned that warm clothes were not needed but sturdy shoes would be a necessity. It was all settled, she was going and now she decided to tell her parents. She had been afraid they would try to dissuade her, but her father was enthusiastic and although her mother did not like the idea, it was probably better than working in a department store.

John met Kathy at Euston and drove her to Heathrow. He warned her that Sudan Airways was OK and he was able to get some complimentary tickets, but they were often delayed and the in-flight food could be described as barely edible. She would be met at Khartoum Airport by Ali the office manager. She was to give him a package that contained documents. John advised that if the customs either in London or Khartoum wished to see them it was OK. Finally, John asked her to send him her thoughts after a few weeks and she could be as honest as she liked.

As John and Kathy approached the Sudan Airways desk, she was amused by the amount of luggage surrounding the other passengers. Kathy only had a small suitcase and a carrier bag. John explained that hand luggage was not a concept understood by Sudanese and over-weight charges were a big source of the Sudan Airways' profits.

As she was leaving John said, "You will need lots of luck and patience but give Sudan a chance; we can do lots of good there. Don't try too hard but please try."

The flight to Khartoum was uncomfortable and very noisy. Kathy was surrounded by other passengers' luggage. It was under her seat and under her feet. The Sudanese around her seemed to talk loudly for the whole flight and, as she knew very little Arabic, it was all mumbo jumbo to her. One or two of the Sudanese said a word or two in English but no one seemed to really strike up a conversation. The landing in Khartoum was greeted by a cheer and one of the passengers explained that by the grace of God they were all safe and home. This was a happy landing for most of the passengers but an apprehensive one for Kathy.

Walking from the plane to the airport building was a new experience. It was hot and dusty, so much so it made her eyes water. She was prepared for the heat but not the dust. Inside the terminal she was met by Ali who, after the initial greetings, said, "This is not a job for a girl but Mr John probably knows best."

Ali was a small elderly man in a jalobia, his English was good and Kathy warmed to him immediately. After that shaky start things went smoothly as the customs and immigration were efficient and quick. The baggage reclaim was slow but her small suitcase came through quickly and was probably the smallest piece of luggage on the conveyor belt that could not really be called a carousel. Outside the terminal it seemed slightly cooler and the dust seemed less. Kathy thought that maybe the plane had stirred up the sand on landing; she was soon to find out that blowing sand was the norm. They arrived at the office and Ali apologised that he had not yet been able to secure Kathy an apartment. The office had a bed and was cooled with an air cooler and more importantly there was a shower.

Ali said that he normally started work at seven a.m. but, as it was past midnight, he would come later to allow Kathy to sleep. She did sleep and was woken at eight a.m. by Ali opening the office. Ali provided a breakfast of broad beans with bread, a glass of cold water and a glass of sweet tea. Kathy was not too sure about broad beans for breakfast but they were delicious, and Ali explained there were onions and cumin as well as the beans. Kathy was not worried about onion breath in the morning. After consuming her glass of water Kathy was still thirsty and she drank several more glasses. Ali then explained to Kathy how this aid agency worked.

"We are not a major player in aid in the Sudan but we try to get the most out of aid for the money donated. Thus, we try to keep the overheads low and so we all have low salaries. Mr John gets money to buy food and medicines from donors in the UK; I try to get money from wealthy Sudanese and we do get some. We pay a very small rent on this office, as the building is owned by a donor; I am trying to get an apartment for you from him."

Kathy listened intently to Ali and wanted to ask questions but thought she should wait until she knew more about the operation. She was impressed by Ali's intensity which matched John's enthusiasm.

Ali advised that they should have a look at Khartoum while it was still cool. Stepping out from the office Kathy found it was anything but. The office air cooler had lulled her into thinking it was cooler outside than it was. The office was near the main market, the souk. This was nothing like the market in Birmingham; her initial impression was that this was mayhem. There seemed to be people, cars, buses and lorries everywhere; there were no road or pedestrian rules. A few shops lined the outside of the market but no real stalls; everything was laid out on the ground — food, clothing and household utensils.

After a quick tour of the market Ali asked if Kathy needed anything. Her first request was eggs and then honey. She found that she could not get her thoughts together in any logical order. She put it down to the flight, sleeping in the office and the seeming confusion surrounding her. It took her a couple of days before she adjusted to Khartoum. Her constant desire was to drink water and yet no matter how much she drank her urine was dark and infrequent. Ali advised her to cover up especially when she was not in the shade. He also advised that in his culture women covered their heads, shoulders, arms and ankles. The head, shoulder and arm covering was accomplished by a fine shawl called a tobe. Kathy loved it; it was light, colourful and could be wrapped in various ways. Ali's wife showed Kathy how to wear the tobe and they laughed at how you could wear a mini skirt underneath. Kathy preferred wearing trousers, so she did not worry about displaying her legs and ankles.

Kathy was trying to learn Arabic and Ali advised her that she should initially concentrate on the local dialect as she was not going to use formal Arabic. Every time she tried to speak Arabic, she would get a reply in a sort of English. Ali explained that in the capital all the locals had some English and to know it was a way to improve their lives. Outside Khartoum she would be confronted by less-educated Sudanese whose knowledge of English would be zero.

Ali had word that a ship was coming to Port Sudan with supplies. Ali briefed Kathy about the shipment and how it was to be handled. Kathy was excited; she was going to get involved with the aid distribution. The Port Sudan agent was called Ishag (Ali suggested she call him Issac) and he would organize the transport to a refugee camp on the Ethiopian border. This camp was run by the Sudanese Army who would have to be informed of the shipment and, more importantly, approve it. Kathy was to go to Port Sudan and organize and oversee the aid getting to the camp. She was to be ready at six a.m., and have a few items of clothing and a large container of water. Ali had borrowed a tobe from his wife for her and had advised Kathy that they would be passing through very conservative areas.

Kathy was at the door of the office at six a.m. and up rolled an old Bedford truck that had seen better days. The driver introduced himself as Omar and thank goodness he spoke some English. It was going to be a long drive and Omar gave Kathy a couple of cushions and a bag of tarmia (falafel). He explained that the road out of Khartoum was paved but most of the way was unpaved and some of it very rough. Kathy should warn him if she needed to stop as he might have to drive a while to find a safe place to park. This was all said with a lot of hand waving and English mixed with Arabic. Kathy liked Omar and she had to put her faith in him as the whole day he would be in charge.

Omar was correct. The road out of Khartoum was paved but then the tarmac seemed to shrink and all the trucks wanted to occupy the middle of the road. Kathy closed her eyes during many near misses but Omar was enjoying the combat. The tarmac ended and then the unsurfaced road began, at first it was smooth but dusty. Then the surface became rippled and finally badly rutted. Kathy was bouncing around in the cab and there was nothing she could hold. After a few hours she asked

Omar to stop and he drove a short way and then he pulled over into the desert.

Kathy dragged herself from the cab and lay down in the sand, which was more comfortable than her seat. All her body seemed to ache and her legs felt like lead. As she lay in the sand, she watched Omar light a small gas stove and boil some water. He was making tea as though they were out for a picnic. A glass of sweet tea revived Kathy and several glasses of water quenched her thirst. She now had a chance to look around; there was little or no vegetation and although they were only yards off the track, she could see no other vehicles.

John's words came back — *try*; she was in the desert a long way from who knew where and she had to try — what else could she do? Omar suggested that if she needed privacy, he would be on the track side of the truck. Kathy smiled to herself, she had not thought about a pee, or the other, but Omar's suggestion had produced an urge.

They set off again and the almost empty truck bounced up and down and Kathy bounced around as well. Kathy had noticed the only cargo in the truck was three sacks of dates and a sack of tea. She asked Omar and was told these were bribes (he called them gifts) for the camp guards. They will ferment the dates and make a drink and of course tea is a staple of their diet; hopefully there would be sugar in the cargo coming in by ship. Omar always seemed to know more than she did, so she asked him how long he had worked for the organization. Omar and Ali had worked with Mr John when he was in the Sudan. After Mr John set up the aid organization, he and Ali were employed as founder members. They had been working together for about ten years. Omar had been Mr John's driver, so when they bought a truck, he became the main driver. His ambition was to go to the UK to visit Mr John. Kathy saw that John was held in high esteem by Omar and Ali and she would have loved to send them to the UK, but on her salary, there was no chance.

Finally, in very late afternoon they reached Port Sudan. The whole town was gloomy, there were no street lights and most of the houses were dark. They stopped at a house surrounded by a high wall and Omar banged on the gate. A tall fully-bearded man in a white jalobia opened the gate. After an extensive greeting Issac came to the point.

"We have had a power cut for two days and I am sorry to tell you that our over-head water tank is empty and an easy shower may have to wait until tomorrow. We do have buckets of water and a ladle so you can tip water over yourself. I am sorry the water is cold."

Kathy so wanted a shower as there seemed to be sand everywhere. The other thing she noticed was that she had started to sweat; Port Sudan was humid unlike everywhere else she had been in Sudan. As they entered the house, she was greeted by Issac's wife Hanan, she offered Kathy a clean set of clothes and suggested that with humid hot air she would need another change in the morning. The water in the buckets was very cold but she enjoyed letting the water dribble over her body. Bathing this way was not as good as a shower but there seemed some satisfaction in directing the water to where it was needed. After the shower she dressed and was greeted by a table full of food illuminated by an oil lamp. Although she had not eaten for most of the day, she was not really hungry just tired. The food was delicious and Kathy excused herself by saying she was too tired to eat but tried a few dishes. Sleep was a problem; although she was exhausted, she was still hot and sweaty and so her sleep was erratic. In the morning she wanted to stay in bed but heard noises from below and thought she should get up. At breakfast she could now eat and the beans were delicious if a little bit peppery. Hanan offered her a fresh set of clothes and although they were a slightly too big for Kathy she was pleased at the looseness in the hot humid air. Issac said that he had heard they might get power later in the day, but he wanted to take her to the harbour. As they drove through the town, she realized there was not much to it except the port. There were lots of single-story houses and a few two-story houses but no high-rise buildings.

On arriving at the port Issac went to see the harbour master and left Kathy surveying the dock. A man approached her and asked if she had cargo she wished to clear. He was a very handsome man who spoke excellent English and she wished he could help her, but she explained she was waiting for a ship with aid. He introduced himself as Bill; that was his English name; his mother was English and his father Egyptian. His parents lived in Cairo and if ever she visited Cairo she could stay as long as she wished. Kathy was starting to want to visit Cairo. In a few minutes she knew much more about Bill than he did about her.

Issac returned from the harbour master and shook hands with Bill. They were regulars in the harbour and knew each other well.

"What does the harbour master say?" asked Bill.

"The ship should dock late this afternoon but probably not unload till tomorrow morning. Our cargo will be loaded onto the trucks which will leave at dawn the next day. I hope the power comes back as Kathy needs a shower."

"I have a generator and Kathy could shower at my place."

At that very moment the power came back, Kathy was a little disappointed as she had been looking forward to the shower. Bill said he would meet them later in the afternoon. Issac and Kathy went back to Issac's house where Issac briefed Kathy on her coming adventure.

"The camp is near the Ethiopian border and with seven loaded lorries will take at least two days and, if you get a sand storm, maybe three. All the drivers know the route so you should not get lost. On each lorry you will have an armed policeman; they love this duty as they get more pay, which of course comes from our organization. The camp is an open camp run by the army. People come and go as they please, but many have walked hundreds of miles. The harvest has been bad and so when they arrive many are starving. You will see mainly women and children. If you see men, they will generally be old. On this trip Omar's lorry will have medical supplies and the other six trucks will have food. If you get stopped let the police do the talking. You may have to use a few sacks of grain but inshallah there will be no problem. Do you have any questions?"

"What do I have to do?"

"You are our representative; you will keep the inventory of all that we supply to the camp. You will take a copy to the Khartoum office. You will have to make decisions that we cannot foresee. Your presence is vital so that the refugees and the army can see someone in charge and as a woman that may be especially important." That last statement was prophetic.

After the long arduous journey and the lack of amenities Kathy's spirits brightened. Issac had just given her a pep talk; now she was ready.

Kathy watched the ship unload. In the company of Bill, she was happy. He had a lot of the cargo to clear, he winked at Kathy as he confided that this would do his bank balance no harm. Issac checked their cargo and asked Kathy to counter check what was loaded onto the trucks. Kathy was a bit bemused at the amount of tinned goods. Issac explained that these were a most welcome addition to the refugees' diet. They could never get fresh meat and the tinned meat was important to their diet. The tinned vegetables may not be exactly to their liking, but hungry people will eat almost anything. The tins would be used to make toys or kitchen utensils and the cardboard boxes would have a multitude of uses. The grain sacks would be highly prized, as the European sacks were of good quality and could be used as mattresses or even to make clothes. The rope through the sacks would have plenty of uses. Nothing would be wasted.

Kathy realized the importance of the aid but she was wondering how she could play an important role in this organization. She could see how committed Ali, Omar and Issac were and she had to try to be as dedicated.

The trucks rolled out of Port Sudan at six in the morning just as dawn was breaking. Visually this was a magical time and Kathy had a ring-side seat. Omar explained that after leaving Port Sudan the road could be very rough, but with fully laden trucks she would not bounce around too much, also the trucks would be going slower than her on trip from Khartoum. The first day they hardly saw a soul except when they passed a few villages. Luckily the locals only wanted to wave, and Kathy was hoping no one came to their caravan begging for food. There were a few stops for prayers, tea and food and then at dusk they halted for the night. The trucks formed a U shape and a couple of the policemen were posted as sentries. Kathy was tired and she slept in the cabin with a pillow for her head; she had a good sleep.

They started just after dawn, after the morning prayers. The day was uneventful until they got close to the camp, when there seemed to be a lot of people on the road, mainly women and children. Omar pointed out that the people were either heading to the camp or leaving it. As they approached the camp Kathy could see an enormous number of tents and only one or two buildings. This camp was in the middle of a desert; Kathy could see no trees or vegetation. The buildings were surrounded by barbed wire and guards. Omar directed the other six lorries to a building that was the store. Omar pointed out that another building with barbed wire was the bakery. Both buildings had armed guards.

They headed for another building with some barbed wire, guards and a queue of women and children. On closer inspection most of the women looked like skeletons and the children were not much better. The truck stopped at the gate and a tall man in a white coat appeared. He introduced himself as Sherif, the army doctor. Kathy introduced herself as in charge of the aid they had brought to the camp.

"I am not yet fully qualified, as I am in my third year of study, but I am also in the army so I am the local doctor."

"This is my first aid trip and I hope the goods we have brought will be useful."

"You cannot know how important this aid is for this camp."

As he greeted her the queue all started to bow and mutter something Kathy could not understand.

"Why are they bowing?"

"They say you are an angel and you have bought them food from heaven."

"I am not an angel and this food is aid for refugees."

"Do not tell them that, to them you are an angel and they really need one."

"Oh, I am not really sure what I should do."

"Just nod at them and put your hands as in prayer."

Kathy did as Sherif had told her and the whole crowd said something she could not understand. They entered the surgery and Sherif asked his helpers to tell the waiting queue that he needed to talk to the angel. "They will all understand, and it gives me a short break. The medical supplies you have brought are so needed as we are running short of almost everything. The commandant has gone to Khartoum to plead for more supplies and even if he is successful it could take weeks to get here. Most of the people in this camp have walked hundreds of miles and when they get here they are starving. Their condition brings on all sorts of medical conditions and I am always struggling to keep them alive."

"Can we go outside for a breath of fresh air? I am sorry but I feel a bit overwhelmed. I can't quite get over this reception."

"Yes, I will order some tea and we can relax on the veranda."

Outside the crowd had built up and they were all bowing. Sherif explained that many of them were Christians and the Muslims also believed in angels. Like it or not, Kathy was the centre of attention and she was overwhelmed.

After a few sips of tea, Sherif excused himself as the queue to see him was getting very long. "Would you like to talk to one of my female Ethiopian assistants called Saha (you can call her Sarah)."

Kathy said, "I hope she speaks English."

Sherif called Sarah onto the veranda and in walked a tall slim woman; she was very good looking. Sarah greeted Kathy in perfect English and Kathy was taken aback.

"Where did you learn English? You speak it so well."

"I was a student at Addis Ababa University studying English language and literature. My family were having trouble on the farm and when my brother died, I had to return to help my parents and sister-in-law. Our plot of land was not large and when the crops failed, we decided to walk to Sudan. It was several hundred miles and both of my parents died. My sister-in-law and I reached the camp but within two weeks she died, so I am alone. I think I survived because I had a better diet in Addis Ababa. I have a sister in Khartoum and hope you can take me there."

"Heavens! That is quite a story but I am not sure if we can legally take you to Khartoum. I will have to talk to Sherif and Omar, who is the lead driver of the convoy."

Kathy entered Sherif's office and all the patients started bowing again — all a little unnerving. She told Sherif about Sarah's request and asked his advice.

"This is an open camp, so Sarah could just walk out and try to hitch a ride to Khartoum. She would not do that as it is not safe, but with you she would feel safe. I am currently in charge of the camp and I could not stop her leaving. There is nothing here for her, actually I would be happy if you would take her."

Kathy found Omar supervising the emptying of his truck. When she told him about Sarah he was surprised and hesitant. Kathy decided it was a decision she must make herself. As she walked to the store, she was sure that taking Sarah to Khartoum was the right one. Everyone was bowing to her and even the guards were smiling and nodding their heads. She entered the store to find the man in charge and to see how the unloading was going. She found a sergeant who was holding a list and assumed he was in charge. As she approached, he was beaming a broad smile and nodding his head politely. Kathy noticed the sacks of dates and tea were put to one side and as she walked towards them, he said,

"Thank you, madam." His English was limited but his smile portrayed his feelings.

Kathy slowly walked back to the hospital and tried to put her thoughts in order. She had not yet told Sarah the good news. Sherif informed her that Sarah was in the hospital wing and that he could send for her, but Kathy decided she would find Sarah herself. As she entered the hospital wing the odour was so intense, she wanted to stop breathing. Sarah saw her and took her straight outside to the fresh air, explaining that all the patients in this ward were close to death. Kathy had never experienced anything so bad before and felt like she would vomit. She sat for a while to get her breath and then asked Sarah how she could cope with that hell.

"These are my people and they came here starved; even though they are dying we give them some medicine to ease the pain and food to ease the hunger. All I can do is wish them a good place in heaven. I am not very religious but I am telling them what they want to hear. I would like to be here to give them comfort, but I would like to be far away not to see the suffering."

"Sounds like you are the angel not me. Surely angels don't want to vomit."

"You are a special angel. You are different and came here of your own free will to give — that is what an angel should do. Everyone in the camp knows your name but they may have difficulty pronouncing it. Newcomers to the camp will be told about you and some will go back to my country and your fame will spread. Dr Sherif was correct when he said they need an angel."

The next day they departed at dawn and almost the whole camp was there to wish them a good journey. Sherif hoped they would all meet in Khartoum and the sergeant from the store was toasting them with a glass of something! The six lorries headed back to Port Sudan and Omar informed them that it would take two days to reach Khartoum with plenty of rough road.

Kathy and Sarah did not notice the rough road, as they chatted about England, Ethiopia and numerous other subjects. Omar concentrated on driving and was almost oblivious to the information passing to and fro. Sarah wanted to know more about life in England; she had read Dickens and Bernard Shaw but knew little about twentieth-century UK. Sarah was fascinated by George Orwell and particularly about animals with human traits, a concept almost anti-religious. Kathy was out of her depth with literature and had to resort to describing everyday life in the UK.

The first day passed very quickly and after a few stops they were camping for the night outside a small village. Omar explained they could buy a few provisions here and then the village would protect them. Kathy wondered who could attack them in this desert but Sarah informed Kathy that they had a truck, fuel, food and possibly jewellery, a tempting prize.

The journey to Khartoum was long but as they approached the city, Kathy began to think of what to do with Sarah. Omar said he knew of an area south of the city where many Ethiopians lived, in an industrial area. There were no addresses and no organized streets, but he could drop Sarah on the main road and then she was on her own. Kathy wrote the address of the office and Ali's name and pleaded with Sarah to get in touch. Kathy was going to try and find her a job.

Arriving back at the office, Kathy had a lot to tell Ali and a report to send to John. After telling Ali about the whole episode she concentrated on Sarah and hoped Ali could find her a job. The report to John was short but to the point.

The trip to Port Sudan and then to the camp was horrendous and she had almost resigned. She had bounced around in trucks and her whole body ached.

Ali, Issac and Omar were so dedicated to the organization that it would collapse without them.

Being called an angel had an effect she could not describe but helping people in distress and near death had been overwhelming. She now realized the necessity for aid.

Furthermore, Kathy had made a friend of a refugee who was more educated than she and that was humbling.

John was delighted with Kathy's short report and an educated refugee was an important selling point to sponsors.

Ali was impressed with Kathy's performance on her mission. He was also impressed with her decision to bring Sarah to Khartoum. All refugees arriving in Khartoum could have a very difficult time. Female refugees would be exploited and both males and females could be enslaved. If they were lucky, they might be taken on as servants but other forms of servitude such as prostitution were available. Ali was alive to these possibilities but kept them from Kathy. He could never discuss such things with a woman, not even his wife.

Ali had so many contacts in Khartoum he assured Kathy he could find Sarah a job. In the meantime, he had acquired a flat for Kathy in the centre of Khartoum. It was very basic with poor furniture, but there was one bedroom, a kitchen, a living room and a bathroom with a shower. Kathy giggled when she heard the word shower as it reminded her of the bucket and scoop in Issac's house.

Sarah came to the office and after Ali heard her speak, he said they should go to the British Council. The librarian was so impressed with Sarah's knowledge of English and literature, he could offer her a part-time job. Ali had contacts in the Ethiopian Embassy, and they were able to get Sarah's transcripts from Addis Ababa University. Sarah said that the area where her sister lived was very bad. Kathy invited Sarah to live with her and she could keep the place clean and tidy as Kathy would be away for long periods.

Kathy had various trips to refugee camps on the Ethiopian and Chad borders, but the first camp was her favourite. Each time she visited that camp they all came out to greet her. The first time the refugees had been silent and just bowed but on Kathy's second and third visits the women would ululate and clap. Each time Kathy was overwhelmed with emotion and had to hide her tears. Sherif was still in charge and the camp was no longer an open camp, as the army had brought in more soldiers to stop the refugees getting further into Sudan.

The visits to Port Sudan were very pleasant especially with a dinner at Bill's house. Kathy got to meet his parents who were visiting from Cairo. Bill wanted to propose but she told him to wait as she wanted to do more for refugees. When Kathy went on a short leave she stayed with Bill's parents in Cairo, who treated her like a daughter.

Sarah was now in demand. The British Embassy employed her occasionally for translation work and another aid agency wanted her to visit some camps on the Ethiopian border. The problem with travel was her lack of a passport and a Sudanese resident visa. To Ali that was a challenge and he set about using all his contacts to get the passport and visa.

One night as Kathy and Sarah were having dinner, Sarah got very teary and serious.

"I am not religious, but you are an angel and Ali is one too."

"I am no angel."

"Let me finish. If you had not agreed to bring me to Khartoum, I would still be in that camp and possibly dead. Sherif is trying his best, he is probably another angel, but that camp is a death place. Bringing me to Khartoum gave me possibilities I had never imagined. Ali has worked wonders and you have shared your life with me. I now have work, money and self-esteem. I am able to support my sister and teach her English. I hope in the future to help my people in other camps, I have met a very nice Coptic Sudanese and am thinking of marriage."

"That is news to me — where and when?"

"You remember when you took me to the Sudan Club as a guest; that is where. When, was a few months ago. You have been out of Khartoum many times and I needed company. Another development is that Mr John is trying to get me a scholarship to a British university. My life is like a fairy tale and I cannot thank you enough."

Kathy was also thinking of marriage but she wanted to make more people happy; her own happiness could wait. She was to go to Juba and supervise the distribution to camps and hospitals in South Sudan. Supplies came by road from Kenya and by air from Nairobi and Khartoum. Most of the medical supplies went to hospitals in and around Juba. Some of these hospitals were run by Brits and other Europeans. In general, the medical supplies came by air but the food supplies came by road, often through rebel territories. Ali had been in touch with Colonel Garang who was the leader of most of the rebel groups. As Kenya was a 'friendly' country to his organization he was persuaded not to interfere with the trucks coming from Kenya to Juba.

Kathy went to Juba and was housed in the British Council compound. This was paradise; she had a well-furnished suite with uninterrupted running water and a swimming pool for her relaxation time. She could prepare her own food or occasionally dine at the Juba Hotel across the road. She soon found that the south Sudanese were very friendly and as a regular at the airport she had her own special chair. Plane times were not always to schedule and a chair in the shade was a necessity. She often visited Juba University and gave a few lectures on English and social science. Kathy was not too bothered by the hot humid environment which was better for her than the hot dry one of Khartoum. There was no club in Juba but there were regular parties of expatriates and locals. Booze was not a problem as before Sharia there were several breweries in the south. Kathy was not a big drinker but enjoyed a cold beer.

Problems started when Colonel Garang was killed in a plane crash. The convoys from Kenya were often attacked and flights into Juba became more erratic as the rebels were reported to have ground-to-air missiles on hills surrounding Juba. Kathy tried her best to contact rebel groups, but they were very fragmented and the Arab truck drivers became scared of bringing goods to Juba. They would go to other towns near the Kenyan or Ugandan borders but would venture no further. Finally supplies slowed to a trickle and Kathy was recalled to Khartoum.

One problem while she was in Juba was the sudden imposition of Sharia law. The leaders in the south had immediately rejected it and, although it did not affect Kathy, she could see a sudden increase in tension in Juba. She would have loved to stay there but the security situation was getting worse and she was resigned to leaving.

Back in Khartoum, Kathy was sent to the Chad border. This was a long road trip through several army check points. The whole area was in turmoil because of the drought and the failure of staple crops. In Chad there was a rebel insurgency and the refugees coming to the camps were starving. Her first convoy could offer only temporary relief and she had to give up some of the supplies to local starving Sudanese. This and subsequent journeys were the hardest times she had endured. Back in Khartoum she admitted to Ali that she was exhausted and was in need of a rest. Ali knowingly sent her to Port Sudan and said she should help Issac clearing and sending food to the camps.

Within one month, Kathy was overjoyed to get married to Bill. Her parents and Bill's, were in Port Sudan for the wedding and previously her parents spent a few weeks in Cairo. Bill and Kathy spent their honeymoon in Nairobi. Sarah received a scholarship to

York University and Sarah's sister became the assistant librarian at the British Council in Khartoum. John and Ali are still trying their best to help refugees.

Sent Home

"I'm being sent home to the States; I know too much and they want to offload me. I volunteered for this job and now I know the truth — I'm being shafted." Glen was almost in tears as he blurted out his problems. As an American in Khartoum he was very visible and that made both Sudanese and expatriates suspicious. Numeri's government had oscillated between the West and the East and both sides had several spies trying to find where Sudan fitted in the world 'camp'. Glen could be one of them.

"Before I came to Africa, this continent was a series of TV pictures implanted in my brain. It was wild animals and scantily clad black people shining in the sun. Nobody prepared me for reality. They didn't lie to me; they just didn't tell me the truth. My interview was a perfect example; Africa was only mentioned in passing; it was all about what I could do. They said it might be difficult, but I would be 'taken care of.' My interviewers had probably never been to Africa, how could they prepare me? They did not know the reality of Africa but now I know, I want to get the truth out. Starving people, unliveable conditions and aid that goes nowhere except into a few pockets." Glen was almost in tears.

Kathy and Glen had met at an expatriate party several months before. There was an afternoon 'tea party' and then those who had more alcoholic drinks would stay for the evening party. Sharia had meant that parties had to be carefully arranged so as not to draw suspicion of the local police. Kathy was not really a drinker and had attended the party to meet new people. Glen could have bought drink from the US Embassy staff, but he was upset that they charged him more money than they had paid. He was also at the party to meet new people. Their mutual interest in the aid programme had brought them together. They did not stay at the party and Kathy took Glen to the Sudan Club. The peaceful surroundings of the club had impressed Glen, he was able to relax for the first time in Sudan. They met a few times in the following months and Glen always wanted to go to the Sudan Club, but this time was different.

Kathy and Glen were sitting on the patio of the Sudan Club; Glen was Kathy's guest. The place was deserted at nine p.m., but before the imposition of Sharia law it would have been full of expatriates enjoying a boozy evening. The total ban on alcohol meant that this night spot was now a dead spot. They were sitting in almost silence, no sound except what they uttered.

The patio locally known as the mustaba was deserted except for Glen, Kathy and a waiter who was standing near the bar. Tonight, it was very quiet; the moon was full and there was no wind and being December, the night air was relatively cool. Glen felt at peace in this place, he was never challenged, accosted or even recognized. This was a place to relax but tonight he could not relax. He was being 'shipped out' and was hiding from his 'escorts'. He was spilling out all his emotions to Kathy and hoping no one would find him.

"I came to Sudan believing I could help, believing I was working for an organization that would help. I should have realized the problem when I was met at the airport by a bum who, before introducing himself, wanted to know if I had any booze. The cretin seemed upset when I told him I had been pre-warned of the new Sudanese law. This idiot turned out to be the manager of the Khartoum office. My first reaction was that he was a helpful nerd but now I know better. The guy is a malicious, parasitic turd, one of the crooks I'm going to nail. Can you believe that lots of people are sending money to Africa to support this low life? I wish I could dig a hole in the desert and bury him."

Kathy took a sip of her soft drink and looked at Glen. She understood some of his anger; she worked for an aid agency too and had some similar frustrations but her boss, Ali, was so different. The torment of lives in Africa had been met by a well-meaning response from America and Europe. Money pouring into numerous agencies was supposed to solve the problems, which were bigger than anyone could understand, even an established organization such as Oxfam. Some of the agencies seemed to spend little on actual aid. Her agency was trying to spend little on infrastructure but as much as they could to get help directly to the needy.

"The Sudanese are a beautiful people; here I am treated like a king. Can you believe it, I'm not allowed to pay my own bus fare? I rode the bus from Omdurman to Khartoum and someone paid my fare. I was willing to pay for everyone. I even offered the driver a ten-pound note and he refused it. I still can't believe it. I would rather deal with taxi drivers, at least you know they want to screw you."

Kathy listened while she watched the tears roll down his cheeks. Glen's words reflected her own reality. She allowed him to pour out all his frustrations, and his passion was having an effect on her. Kathy and Glen were lonely people in a strange place, maybe in any other situation they could have fallen in love, but here it was more a sharing of lots of thoughts and frustrations.

"The bastard who met me at the airport took me to an air-conditioned office in the middle of Khartoum and showed me his computer room. He delighted in saying his was the best place in Khartoum; that place is now an obscenity to me. I had no idea what it took to maintain a facility like that in Khartoum, but now I know, I would like to blow it up. A computer facility in the middle of

Khartoum where the hospitals have no medicines, no blood and no fully equipped operating rooms. People queue all night for gasoline, there are frequent power cuts and down the street is a fucking air-conditioned computer room. I went to a barbecue and they had bottled water from Maine, cheese and butter from Wisconsin, bread rolls from Chicago, Polish sausage from Buffalo and I am sure the steaks were imported. The only African thing there was the servants cooking and serving the food."

Kathy breathed slowly through her nose; she was trying to find relief from Glen's emotions. She knew all the problems but felt she had to be a patient listener. Glen was opening up and unashamedly crying and Kathy found she was almost in tears. She was now captured by his anger. Khartoum was a difficult place but she rarely shed a tear.

"They sent me to this camp near the Ethiopian border, the sights made me sick. No one prepared me for the sights and the smells. I was supposed to be a clerk taking goddamn names. I couldn't do it. They were a bunch of starving skeletons and I had nothing to offer them. They made the poor creatures, line up and wait for me to take their names, what for? The poor skeletons could hardly stand and I'm supposed to take their names! After about six names I got up and was sick behind one of the tents. I can still see that sight. Nobody prepared me. I just wanted to get out of there and made the driver take me back to Khartoum."

Kathy had seen similar sights but she was at least able to distribute food. She felt Glen must have been warned and told about the situation. She challenged him, "You must have been told the realities of Africa, some signs, some warnings. Did you not take trucks with food to the camp?"

"I swear to you, Kathy, I was sent there on my own with a driver — an experience beyond anything I could comprehend. In the States I was a city boy, raised in Houston — hot, humid where black and white enjoyed the same hell. I lived in Chicago — hot in summer, very cold in winter, but a big city with lots of facilities. I was not prepared for Khartoum. In the States I was sort of anonymous; here I am so visible. I'm treated like a king, but it is unnerving. I feel I can't do anything to help or change the place; it seems to do something to my self-esteem."

Kathy knew that their skin colour and nationality gave them some privileges but there were some restraints. As a woman in a Muslim society she had to accept the manacles along with the privileges. At least Glen did not face some of the obstacles she felt. Her one advantage was that she could converse with the women and try to understand their problems.

"I get back from that camp and they send me to Juba; I was supposed to work in the south. Now I know they just wanted to get rid of me. Juba is just a big village. I was met at the airport by a man and he apologized for the place. The airport was indescribable

— if you ask me to tell you about it, I will start to giggle. A runway and a few tin shacks and that was it."

Kathy had been to Juba and loved it. One year in Juba was heaven compared with six months in Khartoum. Although it was much poorer than Khartoum, the people who needed her help seemed to appreciate it more. The problem the locals had with dealing with a woman was much less of a problem than in the north.

"I spent a week in that ridiculous place, most of the time by the pool in the British Council compound." Kathy knew that place well. "The refugee camp was not under our 'jurisdiction' and I was told to keep a low profile until things were sorted out. I did wander around Juba a bit, borrowed a Land Rover and drove around the place in ten minutes; there was only about one mile of tarmac road. The whole place runs on tribal lines and there I was representing the white tribe. They treated me politely but with suspicion. I didn't fit. The problem is I really wanted to help but maybe the way to help is to blow the lid off this whole aid scam. After one week by the pool and me feeling like a barbecued chicken, the embassy decided that Juba was a war zone and they shipped Americans back to Khartoum."

Kathy looked at this forlorn figure in front of her, her sympathy draining away, as she was now starting to see him in a different light. Something he had said about the south had triggered something in her, her affection turned to pity. She could not pinpoint her change in attitude but somehow Juba was the key. Glen did not understand the Sudan, Juba or Africa. He suddenly became a threat that could stop help that was needed and Africa sorely needed help. It needed help, unquestioning and unconditional, and exposing a few dishonest tendencies might stop the flow of help. Glen could cause a lot of soul searching that would take time and cost lives. This was too big a price and she longed for his 'escorts' to arrive. Kathy now saw Glen as a snivelling little shit.

"You know what I did when I returned to Khartoum? I found out how much the facility costs. I went through the complete set-up: the rent, the electricity (including what it cost to run the generators), the servants, the cars and drivers, and the expatriate salaries. This adds up to over ninety percent of what is sent to Sudan. Then I found sacks of corn and wheat supplied from America in the market; someone was selling it on the black market. I bet it was the manager. It is all in this letter — give it to some media person, take photocopies and give it to the Sudanese. Give it to anyone who will publish it. I want to expose the bastards. I want to nail them."

Kathy glanced at the document and found Glen's name at the bottom with a PO box number in Houston. She felt sick. She wanted Glen gone out of her life. He was probably going to make money in the US out of his exposé and do damage to all the aid to Africa. Without aid millions might starve. There were many problems including corruption and poor distribution but lots of aid did get through. She was relieved when Glen's escorts came and took him away to the airport without protest. He left without a goodbye, without a whimper, without even a hand kiss, confirming Kathy's negative feelings.

Kathy put the envelope in her purse and vowed not to destroy it, not to use it, but to keep it as a keepsake. She wanted to get back to the realities of Khartoum; she wanted to return to Juba. What she really wanted was the war in the south to stop! The Sudan was a big place she had come to love and it could be destroyed by well-meaning and ill-meaning people, but she would keep trying.

Kathy's Story

After a few years delivering aid in Sudan Kathy felt she was burnt out. Journeys to the Ethiopian border were tough but generally rewarding. Juba had been the easiest time and she wished that she could go back there. The tough times had been delivering aid to the border with Chad. These were long journeys punctuated by lots of check points and hold-ups; the army were not always cooperative and there could be extended arguments and discussions. The army were not totally to blame as they had lots of local problems.

Dealing with starving local Sudanese was the biggest problem. Kathy had to allow for a small loss of her cargo on every trip. Her police escort could do most of the negotiating but she made the decisions. The problem with giving some of the aid was that at the next stop there would be more people requesting food. Information travelled faster than the convoy. The camps on the Chadian border seemed less organized than on the Ethiopian border and she was always happy to leave after the aid delivery.

Ali was aware of the problem and saw how exhausted Kathy was after a trip west. Ali was also aware of the starvation in many parts of Sudan and was trying to decide how much of the aid should go just to Sudan. Even around Khartoum there were several camps of Sudanese, mainly from the south, but also from other areas of Sudan, suffering poor crops due to low rainfall. Several other agencies were trying to provide aid but they were all having difficulty meeting the need. John and Ali were in continual contact and decided Kathy needed a break.

On returning from a trip to Chad, Kathy confided in Ali that she would prefer the next trip to be anywhere else. Kathy understood that the need for aid in that region was great, but it was so difficult. Ali said she should relax in Khartoum for a week or so and he would sort something out. He advised her to go to the Sudan Club and relax. Relax in the pool she did; the quiet around the club was therapeutic. Sharia had had a drastic effect on the club. Members only came for the meals, primarily lunch, and in the evenings the place was almost deserted. Kathy thought this was great; her flat was within walking distance and at night it was cool, as long as you stayed well away from the radiant heat of the concrete buildings.

While in Khartoum Ali arranged a couple of trucks to take food to camps on the outskirts of Omdurman. Omar would drive Kathy to the area, and she would have to decide how the food was distributed. Kathy had not done the distribution before and this was hard. The first camp was populated mainly by south Sudanese, mainly Dinka. Having been in South Sudan Kathy realised she must find a Dinka elder who spoke English and try to let him control the food distribution. Omar was a bit reluctant to take his lorry into the camp, but Kathy persuaded him that if it were stolen then it would be replaced (an offer without substance). Kathy walked into the camp alone and knowing a few greetings and lots of 'pidgin' she was able to find someone speaking English. She found the elder she was looking for and told him her problem. This man was homesick and talked a lot about going home but agreed that many families were close to starving. He had three sons and two of them worked as night guards, so they were not starving but barely getting by.

The old man advised that the trucks should not come into the camps as there would be a riot. He would ask the desperate families to have carts or some sort of carriers at the edge of the camp. The lorries should have some police available in case of trouble and he and his sons would unload the lorries and give something to the deserving families. He warned Kathy to be far away in case of trouble. Kathy realized that this was a lawless place unlike other camps she had supplied, so sad being so close to Khartoum. The first trip went well but word spread, and subsequent trips were more chaotic. Ali decided to employ an educated Dinka to control further food distributions.

Back in London, John was getting some backing from European companies. They were interested in his quiet approach to aid and were not too enamoured with the antics of some aid agencies. Most of the aid was now going through Port Sudan and John decided that Kathy could be of help in there. Actually, Ali had first suggested that Kathy could be of help in Port Sudan. Ali was very good at understanding and assessing people; his dealings with his compatriots and the expatriates showed that he could have been a diplomat if he had had the contacts.

Ali's suggestion that she should go to Port Sudan was greeted with great delight by Kathy. Port Sudan had two attractions: Bill and Issac's family. Bill was a romantic attraction but Issac and Hanan were special friends. Kathy always remembered how well they welcomed her despite the lack of electricity and water. Hanan had given her clothes and given her lots of good advice. She had stayed with them several times and their quiet hospitality always had Kathy astounded. Kathy felt completely at home in their house.

Port Sudan was growing but even with a large population still felt like a village. There were a few expats in a very Sudanese town. Kathy was immediately identifiable and in general was treated very well. She was staying with Issac but had a lot of contact with Bill. Issac warned Kathy that even though she was a Christian, under Sharia she had to be careful about being seen with a man who was not her relative or husband. During these discussions she learned that Issac was a Christian but Hanan was a Muslim.

Bill and Kathy met regularly on the docks and they loved each other's company. Bill finally (he had tried before) proposed. Kathy was now resigned to no more adventures to Chad and accepted. She wanted to continue with the aid work but realized that the only way she could be with Bill was as his wife. Issac was very much in favour of their marriage; locally everyone regarded Issac as Kathy's guardian and he should protect her reputation. Locals around the docks knew and liked Kathy and the local police were very appreciative of the extra pay they received when aid was transported. Even her angel status had reached Port Sudan.

Arranging the wedding was not simple. Bill was a Copt and there was a Coptic church in Port Sudan. Coptic weddings tended to be several hours long and quite complex. Bill and Kathy had to negotiate with the priest for the simplest and shortest form he could manage. Then there was the problem of the guests. Both sets of parents had to be invited; Issac and Hanan were a must and then Ali and Omar from Khartoum. John was invited from London, but he declined excusing himself with too much work.

Bill's parents were over the moon. They had thought that Bill would never find a suitable wife in Port Sudan. Kathy's parents were equally excited as they had wondered if Kathy was going to finally get a husband. It was decided that before the wedding both sets of parents should meet in Cairo. Kathy and Bill would also travel to Cairo by air, an excellent meeting place as Bill's parents had a large house able to accommodate everyone. Kathy was a bit apprehensive about her parent's reaction, but she should not have worried; her mother was enthralled with Cairo and her father loved just seeing history right in front of him. Bill's parents loved having new people staying who were enjoying their lives and they were happy with Kathy, who was mature and intelligent.

They all had one week in Cairo where Kathy's parents enjoyed a tour such that no tour guide could have given them, with so much local knowledge. They visited the Pyramids early in the morning before the local distractions were awake (no sellers and people trying to let you ride their camels or donkeys). They visited the City of the Dead before the tourists got there. The visit to the Cairo museum had Kathy's dad in ecstasy. Kathy's mom could hardly contain herself as they drank coffee on the Nile at sunset. Kathy had wondered how her parents would cope with Cairo but now she was wondering how she could extract them to Port Sudan. Kathy's father was even talking about moving to Cairo.

Bill had been relaxed; he knew that his parents would accommodate their visitors but even he was taken aback by how well they mixed. Bill's dad was a very educated Egyptian and spoke perfect English. His interests were in politics and history, which almost matched the interests of Kathy's dad. Bill's mother was interested in cookery and Kathy's mom was a good cook. The parents seemed to be more suited than Kathy and Bill. Bill noticed how excited his father had become and how proud he was of his home town. The dinners were feasts and both mothers were having fun producing exotic meals together. One week passed so quickly but the wedding was approaching.

They all arrived from Cairo on the same flight and Issac had arranged transport from the airport. Kathy had seen very little of Port Sudan which was much bigger than she had previously thought. Moving out of the city in her aid convoys meant she had only seen a small part of the city. She remarked to Bill that this was more than a small village. He laughed and said that the population was growing quite fast and this was becoming one of the biggest cities in Sudan.

Bill had arranged to house both sets of parents in his house; Kathy was to stay with Issac and Hanan. After the airport the first stop was Issac's house so that they could all meet Hanan, who had plenty of food waiting. Kathy's dad enjoyed the mezza and just loved the fried kidneys and the hummus. Kathy's mom was a bit choosier but enjoyed a few dishes and asked for recipes from Hanan, who was delighted and said she would supply any recipe required. The only thing missing was a beer or wine to wash the food down. Kathy had to explain Sharia to her dad but confided that Bill would have something at his house.

Bill did have a few refreshments at his house, and they imbibed into the early hours. The next day Bill took Kathy's dad to the dock and explained how he made his living. This was impressive and Kathy's dad marvelled at the amount of cargo on the dock. Bill explained that many of the owners came from Khartoum taking one or two days to get to Port Sudan to remove their cargo. Meanwhile the mothers were having a good chat about their respective children, as mothers do.

Kathy was at Issac's house putting the finishing touches to her wedding dress; that Hanan had made. The dress was quite modest and covered much more of Kathy's body than might be expected of a summer wedding dress in the UK. Kathy appreciated Hanan's effort; Kathy was regarded as a daughter and everything was done with pleasure. Kathy told Hanan she was a little apprehensive about marriage and how it would affect her life. Hanan was reassuring and told how, despite all the difficulties in her marriage, she and Issac just made it work. Both sets of parents (Issac's and Hanan's) had been very reluctant to welcome the marriage, and they had all expressed the view that it would not last. Hanan's parents had been somewhat swayed by Issac's business acumen and Issac's parents had been swayed by Hanan's ability to make a good home for Issac. Many of Hanan's conservative relations had shunned her but as time went by, they relaxed their views. Hanan observed that Kathy would have no problem with her parents and in-laws.

Ali, his wife Salah, and Omar with his senior wife Ahwadi arrived in a newish Land Rover and there was an extended greeting performance. Sarah sent her apologies as she was still awaiting her passport and without ID there could have been a problem if she had been stopped at a check point. Salah was well known to Kathy but Ahwadi was not. Ali and Omar left the women alone to get to know each other. Kathy knew many Sudanese words and phrases, but deep conversation was difficult. There was lots of translation and laughter, but Kathy did learn that Ahwadi was one of two wives and the children (seven of them) had been left with the second wife. Kathy had been in Sudan several years but had never thought seriously about polygamy. Now she was getting married she wanted to know more and here was a first-hand participant. Hanan was quick to explain that Issac could not take another wife, but if she had married a Muslim man, she could have been one of four wives depending on how prosperous her husband was.

Kathy had never considered the marriages of other women in Sudan. Hanan explained that in the home, and particularly in the kitchen, the wife was queen. The wife could entertain other women and the man could entertain his male friends. In conservative households there would be no mixing but in more liberal society there could be some mixing. Ahwadi was not well educated and would never expect to have a conversation with any man but her husband. Salah was more educated but would need her husband present when having a conversation with another man. Even though Hanan was less strict in her attitudes, she still preferred to have Issac there when other men were present. Talking to Kathy and Bill's dads was easy as their wives were present, but she would have been shyer in the absence of the women. Hanan did admit that talking to foreign men was easier than talking to Sudanese men.

Kathy was enjoying this frank discussion of male—female relationships and was happy that Bill, being a Copt, could not take another wife. Ahwadi explained (interpreted by Salah) that Omar was a good husband and she loved his second wife. The two wives could share all the chores, problems and happiness. Having seven children between them meant they could share all the duties to the children. Omar was away a lot and she had company. Kathy had a problem with the concept of two wives but was starting to see a few advantages. Ali only had one wife, Salah, but if he had a need to have a second wife, they would discuss it and she would probably agree. Her mother was one of four wives and so she had a real mother and three other mothers.

After a couple of hours Ali and Omar returned. Ali had met some relatives and they now had accommodation for the night. The ladies had discussed married life in detail and as Salah and Ahwadi left there was lots of hugging and kissing (between the women of course). After they had gone Hanan admitted to Kathy that she had not expected the two women to speak so freely about marriage. She thought that maybe Omar had told his wife to give Kathy lots of advice.

Later Issac, Bill and Kathy's dad arrived with two strangers who were introduced as the consuls of Egypt and Italy. The consuls were on a fact-finding mission. The Egyptian consul was a friend of Bill and his father. The Italian consul explained that there were several Catholic schools in Sudan and as a representative of the Italian Government he wanted to meet the priests and ask what they needed. Even in north Sudan the Catholic schools were well attended, although many of their pupils were Muslim. In South Sudan there were many Catholics and a need for more schools.

Kathy was happy to see Bill and they escaped to the kitchen while the others chatted. They had not had any time together since they arrived from Cairo. Bill was apologetic that he was having a better time than Kathy. She explained that the female discussion she had recently entered into was fun and informative; she would not have missed it for the world. She was very happy to see Bill for the last time before the wedding.

After the visitors had left, she decided to have an early night and went straight to the shower. Entering her bedroom in the nude she took a long look at herself in the mirror. She never stood for any length of time in front of the mirror but now she was looking at what Bill would see. No one else had seen her fully naked since she was about fourteen. Bill had always seen her fully clothed and the only time she had been partially undressed was in the pools in Juba and at the Sudan Club. On both occasions there were very few people around and no one she really knew.

She had very white skin; it had rarely been exposed to the sun in Sudan and never in the last month. Her breasts were firm, not too big and not too small. Her hips were a reasonable size and her bum was not too big, but she was still anxious what Bill would see. They had kissed and cuddled and Bill had kissed her neck and shoulders but they had not been intimate; she was still a virgin. Before coming to Sudan, Kathy had a few short relationships but they had not gone far, possibly because she had refused to have intercourse. She had not been with a man well before she had come to Sudan. Of course, she had not seen Bill naked, but he was bound to be OK. But would she be?

Salah tried her best to calm Kathy's nerves on her wedding day. Putting on her new wedding dress seemed to be difficult, although the last time she had tried the dress it was perfect. She was sweating more than normal and Kathy had no appetite for breakfast. Salah was smiling to herself; these were what she called 'freedom lost to a man'. Issac arrived with Kathy's father and suddenly Kathy was at peace. Issac and Salah would go on ahead and a car would soon arrive to take Kathy and her father to the church.

Kathy's father was in an elated mood.

"Last night was the best evening I have ever spent. Those two consuls were just magnificent and the stories they told were incredible; they knocked your mother's socks off. Their English was perfect and their knowledge was astounding. We wanted them to stay longer but it was getting late. By the way, how are you?

"I am a bit nervous, but do you think I am doing the right thing?"

"You are my only child, my only daughter; if I could find fault in the man you were to marry, I would tell you so. You know Bill better than I but what I see is someone I would be proud to have him as a son-in-law. Your mother and I had wondered whether you would find a suitable man but we both agree you have won the lottery."

The car arrived and they were whisked off to the church. Omar and Ahwadi wished them well outside the church, but apologised as they could not enter. Inside the church there were just a few strangers Kathy's dad had not met. Kathy pointed out the harbour master, the police chief, two crane operators and three dockers. Kathy's dad thought Bill must be a socialist; he had invited the high and the low. What Kathy's dad did not know was that the dockers were Copts.

They all gathered in front of the altar and the short service began. After a while Bill turned and motioned to the congregation that they should sit. Kathy wished he had motioned to her to sit. Kathy wished Sarah was there to translate and her mind wandered to Sarah. She would understand this mumbo jumbo and would have loved the occasion. Finally, the vows and the commitments, where they both agreed, and they were married. At this stage Kathy felt exhausted but exiting the church into the sunshine she was refreshed. Seeing Omar and Ahmadi patiently waiting outside lifted Kathy's spirits.

The congregation all went back to Bill's place where they had a garden party. There was plenty of food and drink (non-alcoholic). Ali and Omar chatted with Kathy's dad and the consuls left early to continue their tour, a disappointment for Kathy's mom. Bill entertained his other guests while the women went inside to help Kathy get out of her wedding attire. They were all complimenting her and telling her that she had definitely married the right man. As the afternoon rolled into dusk Kathy was getting more nervous. She wanted to be alone with Bill in their bedroom, but what was going to happen?

Finally, the guests left and the family had a quiet drink with toasts to celebrate the marriage. Kathy noticed that Bill's dad had tears in his eyes. Was that a good sign? Maybe Bill was sentimental. Bill was in a very happy mood telling the gathering of his plans for the future. He wanted to earn enough money so that Kathy and he could travel anywhere in the world. He had his mom's relatives in the UK and of course his in-laws. Kathy's dad said he would be proud to show off his new son-in-law down the pub and when he got back to England, he would have many stories to tell. All this banter was passing Kathy by; all she could think about was the bedroom.

The next day they would all be going to the airport, Bill and Kathy to Nairobi, the parents to Cairo. They all agreed to an early night to pack and get ready for tomorrow. This was Kathy's opportunity to speak up. She told them that John had given her a job that was demanding, low paid and exhausting, but she loved it. She had met wonderful people in Sudan and seen sights she could never have imagined before she came to Africa. She had met many lovely people but of course Bill was special. One other special person not present was Sarah, who was currently in Khartoum and not able to travel to the wedding. She jokingly said that she was glad Sarah had not met Bill first, otherwise it could have been a different wedding today. Kathy was letting out her feelings and it felt good; it was reducing her nervousness.

The bedroom was cool but not cold, still Kathy had a little shiver. She stood in front of Bill and blurted out, "I am a virgin."

Momentarily Bill was taken aback, but he sadly replied, "Sorry, I am not." Bill did not elaborate; he did not tell her anything she did not want to know.

"Well I am glad we are not both virgins as we would not know what to do."

"Nature would direct us. Shall we see, maybe we should get undressed and go to bed."

Kathy was so nervous she was naked before Bill had taken off his shirt. Bill stood back and admired her. "You are so beautiful, so white like an angel."

The word angel seemed to embolden Kathy and she said, "Come on get undressed — I want to see my male angel." Suddenly Kathy was relaxed; Bill had looked at her and liked what he saw. Now was the time she had dreaded and hoped for at the same time.

They jumped onto the bad and lay naked together. Bill started by stroking her breasts and arms and then slowly moved down her body.

"Your skin is so soft and smooth to the touch, I'm still feeling for a rough patch."

They both laughed and started kissing. Kathy felt so at ease she could hardly believe how comfortable she felt. Then it started to get a bit more serious and Bill was in the process of penetration. Kathy felt a sudden sharp pain and she winced.

"Shall I stop?"

"No, no, please carry on it was only momentarily painful."

Now he was deep inside her and it was the weirdest feeling. She was taking short breaths as she felt a normal breath might take the feeling away. His rhythm started to increase, and the feeling was getting stronger, then he suddenly gave a grunt with a sigh and stopped. Kathy was confused about what should happen next. As he withdrew there was a sharp pain which made her gasp and he kissed her neck. Then Bill started to stroke her inner thigh. He was so gentle but as he stroked further up Kathy's breathing started to race. Then she felt him touch her clitoris and started to rub it gently.

Oh! This is a different sensation, thought Kathy, it was getting more intense. As he quickened the rubbing action Kathy was starting to give out short sounds. Then she started to shake all over and finally gave out a little cry. Bill stopped and they both relaxed and just lay side by side on the bed.

"That was fantastic. Can we do it again?"

"Let's rest a bit, I need to get my strength back," Bill said laughingly.

They lay there for a while in each other's arms. Kathy was wondering why she hadn't married him months ago; he had wanted to propose and she had stopped him. After a short while Bill climbed on top of her and the process was repeated. The second time was better than the first as she knew what to expect. This time Bill was telling her how beautiful she was and how lucky he was to have her. Kathy could not utter any coherent words; she was so involved in her pleasure.

The next morning, she awoke to a strange sound and realized Bill was having a shower. She had wanted to shower last night but did not want to leave Bill's embrace and had fallen asleep. Bill came out of the shower naked and Kathy could not take her eyes off him; his bronze body was so perfect. He looked at her white body on white sheets and just loved what he saw.

"I must get dressed and prepare breakfast and then we have to get your clothes from Issac's house."

Kathy wanted to say bugger breakfast come back to bed, but she realized her parents and parents-in-law would need to eat.

"I will shower and join you."

Bill found his mother and mother-in-law in the kitchen and they both told him to go relax in the lounge as everything was in hand. He was very happy that they seemed to be enjoying each other's company. His mother had very few friends in Cairo and could not stand most of his father's relatives. Since he had left home, he had learned that most of his father's relatives had been banished from the house and if his father wanted to meet them, he should do so elsewhere. His father understood and so family gatherings were rare. Bill was sure that his mom would be despised in the family, but he was on his mom's side; they were an oppressive bunch.

Kathy entered the lounge to find Bill relaxed on the settee, so she cuddled up to him. She was glad the mothers were preparing the breakfast as she could have more time alone with Bill. That time was short though as the front door opened and in walked their fathers. They had been for a stroll before the sun started to make activity more difficult. Kathy's dad said he would find it difficult to live here due to the humidity, but Bill's dad had told him Cairo was much dryer and the heat more bearable. Bill felt so lucky that both sets of parents were getting on so well; all he had to do was take care of Kathy. Bill was an only child and Kathy was an only child and future life could have been difficult if their respective parents did not get along. Kathy was not thinking about their parents; all she could think of was Bill.

Breakfast was a happy event. Everyone was talking and all were excited about leaving Port Sudan and going their various ways. The parents agreed that the humidity in Port Sudan was tiring but they had all enjoyed the wedding. Kathy and Bill told their parents that they had become used to it and Kathy said she preferred it to the dryness of Khartoum. Bill and Kathy left them to the washing-up and went to Issac's house to get Kathy's clothes.

Issac told them that Ali, Salah, Omer and Ahwadi had stopped by and they were well on their way to Khartoum. They had all enjoyed the wedding and thought that Kathy had found a great husband; Kathy could not agree more. Bill was amused that Kathy did not have a dress other than her wedding dress, which she was not taking. He vowed to buy her a couple of dresses when they arrived in Nairobi.

They all went to the airport in taxis. Port Sudan Airport was not the most comfortable airport in the world, but they did not have long waits for their planes. There was much hugging and kissing when Bill and Kathy took their flight and a promise to visit Cairo in the near future and England later in the year. Finally,

Kathy had Bill alone on the plane and she could snuggle up to him. They did not talk much as she leant upon his shoulder, and the flight seemed to be over too soon. In Addis Ababa airport Bill bought a bottle of champagne and they celebrated their wedding. Now Kathy was flying high and Bill had to settle her down and try to keep her emotions in check. Bill smiled as Kathy fell asleep during the flight to Nairobi; she was not a big drinker.

Kathy did not notice the drive from the airport to the hotel; she was still slightly tipsy and could not take her eyes off Bill. It was a good hotel, but Bill apologised that he could not get a booking in the Norfolk Hotel as it was fully booked. Kathy did not care; all she wanted to do was get Bill in bed.

Bill had hired a car and the first week they spent seeing the safari park, swimming in the hotel pool and enjoying their bed. Kathy also enjoyed the food and going to the market. On the second day Bill had bought her two dresses and a cardigan as Nairobi was cool in the evening. The dresses really suited Kathy's figure and, although she would not be able to wear them in Port Sudan, Bill wanted her to wear them around the house — he liked her legs.

At the end of the week they took the train to Mombasa. Bill explained they could have gone by car but he believed the road was dangerous and he would not risk his prize possession. Whatever Bill said, Kathy could never disagree; he was always right. Again, the train trip was magical. They had a separate compartment and Bill gave a running commentary. Kathy loved the scenery. Mombasa was hot and humid, and Kathy thought it was like Port Sudan. Nairobi had been a bit cool and dry and so Kathy preferred Mombasa. Bill knew Swahili and the taxi to the hotel was filled with conversation between Bill and the driver. At the hotel Bill haggled on the price asked and there was a lot of gesturing and finally a payment. Kathy asked Bill what it was all about. Bill said he was practising his Swahili and had to haggle even though he would have paid the initial asking price.

The hotel had a more Arab feel and Kathy enjoyed the food. Bill seemed more alive than in Nairobi and he explained that this was a place he would like to live. Kathy did not care where they lived as long as she was with Bill. What Kathy did notice was the abundance of Burkas; she had seen very few in Sudan even with Sharia. She also noticed the abundance of fruit and vegetables in the market. When she was in Juba, she had noted the quality of the vegetables coming from Kenya. They had a better time in Mombasa mainly because Bill was enjoying himself more. All too fast the end of the honeymoon was on them and they had to fly back to Port Sudan.

Arriving at Port Sudan they were met by Issac who had some very bad news. The day after their wedding, Ali, Omar and their wives had set off early to get to Khartoum before nightfall. As they approached

Khartoum a truck veered onto the wrong side of the road and smashed into the Land Rover. Omar tried to avoid the crash but he was killed; Ali was injured and so was Ahwadi; Salah was mostly unscathed.

Kathy was in shock. All she could say was "poor Omar". Bill was quick to react, rushing off into the terminal to get two tickets to Khartoum the following day. When he emerged, he found Kathy sobbing on Issac's shoulder. The drive home was punctuated by more bursts of sobbing by Kathy. Arriving home Bill gave Kathy a stiff drink and sat her on the settee. He put his arms around her and said, "We have to be strong for the living."

Kathy started to think about Omar's family. "He has two wives, one of them injured and seven children. How will they cope?"

"We will help them cope. Now get some sleep we are going to Khartoum tomorrow."

Kathy slept fitfully; she was remembering their first trip and how Omar had helped her and looked after her. He had given her space when she needed it, made a difficult journey as easy as possible and instructed his wife to tell her about married life. "Why Omar?" she kept asking herself.

The next day they flew to Khartoum and Kathy was more composed but dreadfully tired. They went straight to the hospital where Ali was staying. Ali was in bed flanked by Salah and Sarah. He had a broken leg, a broken arm and two broken ribs. Kathy held back the tears as she greeted Salah, Sarah and Ali, at least two of them could get hugs. Kathy introduced Sarah to Bill but was at a loss what to say to Ali. Ali was quick to speak after all the preliminary greetings. "Don't worry. I will be out of here in a few days."

"You are staying in here until you are fully recovered and can walk," Salah told him.

Bill smiled to himself, he had never heard a Sudanese wife speak to her husband in such a forthright manner, especially outside the home. Ali took it in good humour and said that his wife knew best. Bill was smiling again as a Sudanese husband had given in to his wife without a whimper. What would he do when Kathy took the high ground?

Sarah now took the initiative and asked if Kathy would like to see Ahwadi, who was in a hospital about two blocks away. Bill could stay with Ali as he would not be allowed to see Ahwadi and they could walk to the other hospital. Sarah took the opportunity of the walk to tell Kathy what was happening.

"I have taken over the office and have spoken to Mr John; he seems a nice man. We have suspended sending aid to the borders but have sent some to camps just outside Omdurman. There is a foreign medical agency working in the camps and we are sending supplies to them. Most of the people in these camps are Sudanese from the south and the west. Mr John agrees with what we are doing. Ahwadi was not badly injured but on the news of Omar's death she was about to give up. Then

Amna, the second wife, came to visit with a couple of children and we persuaded her that she was needed. Amna has been by her side almost every day. I am not sure who is taking care of the other children, but they have told me not to worry."

"You seem to be doing such a good job while I have been enjoying myself."

"It was a struggle, but no one wanted to spoil your honeymoon. I spoke to Issac and he promised he would inform you when you returned. I have been using the office and have installed a computer with the aid of the British Council librarian. He is teaching my sister and me how to use it; I think he likes my sister."

Kathy thought Sarah was a whirlwind, just filling in and doing what was necessary. How could she tell Bill she wanted to stay in Khartoum when Sarah was doing so well?

They arrived at the second hospital which was not as well equipped as Ali's hospital. They were shown to Ahwadi's room where Kathy was introduced to Amna. Ahwadi was pleased to see Kathy and they hugged. Along with Amna were two young children who were staring at Kathy when she hugged Ahwadi. As Kathy approached them, they shrank behind Amna's dress. Amna said something and they both came out with outstretched hands for Kathy to shake. Kathy was really touched, as she had little to do with small children for many a year. Sarah explained that Ahwadi was to leave hospital the following day and Ali had arranged transport for her.

On the way back to the first hospital, Kathy asked if Sarah would mind sleeping in the office while Kathy and Bill slept in the flat.

"Of course not, it is your flat. I would not deprive a married lady of her husband, who by the way is very handsome."

Bill was chatting to Ali when they arrived. Salah had taken the opportunity to go to a nearby market to buy some fruit. Ali had some instructions for Kathy and told her that while his wife was away, he had swayed the doctor into discharging him early. Bill was chuckling to himself; here was a Sudanese man hiding things from his wife and telling another woman.

When Salah returned, Kathy, Bill and Sarah left the hospital and went to the flat. Sarah collected some clothes and left for the office. Bill was amused by the poor furnishings in the flat but did not say anything.

"Sarah is a gem. I love the way she speaks English. She also seems very capable of doing any job that is required of her."

"Yes, she is a gem and I am glad I met you first. She is my best female friend and I hope she 'knocks 'em dead' at York Uni."

"I will stay another day and go back to Port Sudan for a couple of weeks if you don't mind. I have a lot of catching up to do and have to relieve Issac of some of the jobs he has been doing for me."

Kathy was relieved as she was trying to think of how to tell Bill she wanted to stay in Khartoum. She had a good sleep and woke up to find Bill had left the flat. After about twenty minutes he came back with breakfast and the most beautiful and expensive tobe. Later they walked to the office passing many traders who knew Kathy. Word had spread that she was married (probably Sarah had told them) and there were many greetings and well wishes as they passed.

"You must be popular, everyone seems to know you."

"No, I am just friendly." Kathy was very pleased with the reception though and she was enjoying showing off her new husband.

In the office Sarah was hard at work planning a convoy to the Chadian border; Bill was intrigued by the computer. He had thought to buy one when he was last in Cairo and now regretted not having done so. At noon Kathy said they should all go to the Sudan Club for lunch. Bill had never been to the Sudan Club although he had a British passport, and Sarah was keen to see if her 'friend' would be there. Kathy took great pleasure in showing Bill around the club but she admitted that its days were numbered. They all had a lunch of fish and chips and Bill enjoyed chatting with the staff. Bill jokingly said that he wanted to go to England to see if the fish and chips were as good there.

The next day Bill left, and Kathy and Sarah planned the next shipments. Sarah had her passport now and was keen to visit a camp on the Ethiopian border but she also wanted to make plans for her journey to the UK. She had never flown and was a little bit nervous about the journey. Kathy tried her best to reassure her and was tempted to say she should try a flight to Port Sudan but thought better of that idea. Kathy spoke to John on the phone and he was so impressed by Sarah that he could not wait to meet her.

Finally, Ali was out of hospital and was in the office at the first opportunity. Bill arrived and they all saw Sarah off to the UK. They also met Sarah's 'friend', he was a Copt and a very good looking one. Sarah had decided to get married when she had settled in the UK and he was happy with that decision.

Back in Port Sudan life settled into a routine which she enjoyed, giving her plenty of time with Bill. News from Khartoum and the UK was all good; Kathy was sending money to Ahwadi (through Ali) to help support Omar's family, and Bill was telling her all the time she did not need a salary. Shipments were coming in regularly and Bill was clearing more and more goods, thus earning more money. One day a ship docked with an Ethiopian captain. Bill had met this captain before; he and Kathy were invited to dinner on the ship. The dinner was excellent with the best Ethiopian wine. As the dinner progressed the captain started to talk about Ethiopia, a country going through difficult times but there were a few bright lights, one was an angel to the poor people. Kathy wondered what he meant. The captain said, as he looked at Kathy, "I invited you here to meet an angel."

"I am not an angel, I was only delivering aid."

"I know, and you know that, but my poor country people do not know that, and neither should they. Your story is told throughout my nation and let me tell you, the church is not pleased but they can do nothing about the myth. At first the story was not widely known but our government started sending trucks to bring back people from the camps, to occupy the areas almost deserted. Then the myth took off and now every part of the country loves this angel. The written tradition has been for the educated and the church but in any rural society the oral tradition is what has a hold for the poor people. I want to thank you and toast you for being an angel."

As they left the ship Bill put his arm around Kathy's shoulders. "Looks like half of Ethiopia has an angel, and she is my angel."

"Would you like a second angel?"

"What do you mean?"

Kathy grinned and put her hand on her stomach.

"Are you pregnant?"

"Not sure yet, I have not taken the test but Hanan and I have discussed the symptoms and we think that I am."

"Fantastic, I am so pleased. Now I will have to find another place to live."

Found in Kenya

Alan's adventure in Juba had made him realize how much he missed beer. Friends had told him the best place to go was Kenya; they had this great beer called Tusker. He had no leave until Christmas and that was reserved for going to the UK, but he received word that the government were going to close the university for two weeks due to student unrest. Alan quickly found out how to get to Kenya. Ethiopian Airways flew to Addis Abba then Kenyan Airways flew to Nairobi, and tickets were available at a reasonable price. The Khartoum travel agent was a young Sudanese with a very attractive secretary so visiting their office a few times was no problem. The secretary had been to Kenya and stayed in a resort area called Diani Beach; she could recommend a cheap but decent hotel on the beach as some of the resorts were expensive. Alan left everything to her and was delighted with the final cost.

He could do very little at work as most of the students were locked out. It was difficult to get to work as he had to get through army check points. He decided to stay at home and spend some time at the Sudan Club enjoying the pool. Just before he left for Kenya, the students rioted and two students were killed. Now the university was really shut.

The flight from Khartoum was quite short and it took off and landed on time, a plus one for Ethiopian Airways. Addis Airport was much better than Khartoum Airport and had a bar with beer. The Ethiopian beer tasted good but there was a long layover between flights so Alan decided to have a look at the city. The security guard at the door advised Alan that under normal circumstances the round trip to look at the city would be OK, but there were now at least three military check points on the way to the city and the same coming back; it was possible Alan might miss his flight. It was not only Sudan having problems with demonstrations. Alan had another beer and tried to sleep in one of the chairs. He was awoken by a little light-skinned man, who asked whether he was going to Nairobi, and if so, would Alan take his sister's bag as she had left it behind from the last flight. Alan declined, lying that he had the maximum hand baggage that was allowed. His conscience pricked him, but he did not want any trouble on his short 'beer' holiday.

The flight to Nairobi was short and on showing his British passport he was waved through immigration without any formalities. The taxi ride from the airport showed that this was a lush land with lots of green vegetation. Alan realised that he had missed this green colour only having the brown sand in Khartoum. Alan was enjoying the ride; the taxi was newer and more comfortable than the ones in Khartoum. The driver spoke good English and gave a running commentary on all the sights. As they pulled into the hotel car park, he noticed there was a radio tower nearby, and the carpark was clean and the hotel painted white. This white was only matched by the white of the buildings in the Sudan Club that needed refreshing every year.

After unpacking his trolley bag which basically contained tee shirts, underwear, a pair of sandals and one pair of shorts (he liked travelling light) he went to the bar and tried his first Tusker beer. He went to sit out on the veranda but found the night air quite chilly; he had become acclimatized to Khartoum. Inside the bar it was a bit warmer but smokier. He noticed that there were several single women looking at him and realized they were prostitutes. He was thinking to himself that Sharia would have a field day here. After his second beer he retired to his room and had a good sleep.

The next day Alan had breakfast early and decided to walk to one of the bigger hotels. He had a map and the hotel did not look far. When he got to the gate the guard asked him where he was going and, when Alan named the hotel, the guard told him to take a taxi.

"It does not look far," Alan commented.

"There is a park you must cross and there are many bad people there," replied the guard. Alan decided he would take a taxi but instead of to the hotel he would go to near the centre of town. He was dropped near where he had been told the buses for Mombasa departed. As he was walking, he saw a Sudan Club member having his sandal mended. They chatted for a while and his acquaintance said he should be on guard as many people might offer help and they might not have good intentions. His other piece of advice was to go further down the street and have a look at the market.

Alan strolled down the street until he saw a building with an archway entrance; it looked like a small railway station. On entering the building, he was astonished at the display of flowers. It was so full of colour the contrast from the outside was startling. The rest of the market hall was filled with vegetables and fruit but the flower display was the sight that was etched in his memory.

Leaving the market, he made a mistake. He took out his map to see where to go next. He was joined by a passer-by offering help. The warning from his acquaintance came to mind and he carried on walking, telling this man he did not need help. That did not shake the persistent fellow, so Alan had to find another way out. As they were walking, he saw a restaurant called the Carnivore and Alan said, "Yes, there it is," and walked through the entrance.

He had lost his 'escort' but he was not yet feeling hungry, but he would have a snack. He had heard of this restaurant and when he saw the menu it was truly full of exotic dishes. The waiter was very charming and the restaurant almost empty (it was too early for lunch). Alan explained he only wanted a snack and coffee; the waiter suggested a sandwich of any meat on the menu. Alan decided on an ostrich sandwich and it was delicious. There was some kind of sauce on the meat and it was tender, The taste seemed to be something between a game bird and beef. The coffee was also very good and he ordered a second cup, as this Kenyan coffee was the best he had tasted.

Inside the restaurant he could consult his map and found the buses left for Mombasa almost across the street from the Carnivore restaurant. He talked to the waiter who advised him not to walk more than five hundred yards down the street to the left and to head back to the taxi rank near the restaurant. Alan did as he was told and strolled past several shops with rather large guards with baseball bats. They smiled at him but seemed to scowl at everyone else. He went back to the taxi rank and asked to go back to his hotel. He relaxed in his room for the afternoon and decided to go to another hotel for his evening meal.

The taxi took him a short ride to the hotel across the park. He sat out on the veranda and had a good English meal. It was not a patch on his ostrich sandwich, and he vowed that if there was a Carnivore restaurant in Mombasa he would visit it. As he sat at the table, he felt a bit out of place as most men were wearing long trousers and shirts and he was in shorts and a tee shirt. After he had finished his meal the waiter asked if he would like to take his drink to the bar, as they were expecting a big crowd and they would have to join some tables together. Alan was annoyed and so he finished his drink and left. No one had asked him to move on for years since an upmarket restaurant in England, could there be some kind of hierarchy in Nairobi?

The next morning, he took a taxi to the bus terminus and found the ticket office. The first bus was not full, but all the window seats seemed to be occupied so he decided to sit on the bench seat at the back. He sat in the middle so he could see straight down the aisle and through the front window. This was OK as they slowly made their way out of Nairobi, but when they got on the so-called highway it was a bit scary seeing the traffic coming in the opposite direction. The road seemed to narrow as the tarmac was crumbling at the edges. The oncoming trucks all seemed to want to occupy the middle of the road and, although the bus stayed well on the correct side of the road, there were a few near misses. Alan was now glad it was Mombasa airport he was leaving from in the next ten days' time. He started to notice the wrecked vehicles on the side of the road and started to look for wrecked buses; fortunately, there were none.

As they approached Mombasa the air started to get hotter and stickier; the bus was not air conditioned. They had descended from Nairobi to sea level at Mombasa. With the open windows it had almost seemed as if it were cold in Nairobi, but now the breeze was hot and humid. At least the road became wider and better maintained and the outskirts of the city were very interesting. They started with thatched huts which later became small bungalows then bigger houses followed by a few two- and three-storey buildings. As they entered Mombasa the density of traffic increased manyfold and near the centre it was almost impossible to go more than a few miles per hour. This city seemed more congested than Nairobi and the streets were definitely narrower.

Alan started to notice the Arab influence; the men and women were in flowing robes and a few women were in full length black gowns that covered their head and face with a little grill in the gown so they could see. He could not remember seeing this dress in Khartoum. Women in Khartoum covered their head and shoulders in an attractive tobe which was often highly coloured and almost see through. Mombasa was so different from Nairobi it could be in another country.

Alan was glad to get off the bus into a bus station like no other. There were buses of all shapes and sizes seemingly parked in a haphazard manner. Alan needed a drink, but he did not trust the bottled water sold in the bus area. His bag felt much heavier in this heat, but he soon found a shop calling itself a 'supermarket. In the shop he found a diminutive Indian who spoke very good English and sold him a bottle of water while trying to sell him everything else in the shop. Alan said he was going to Diani Beach and asked where he could catch a matatu. Most of the matatus were mini-buses but some were similar to the boxes in Khartoum. The Indian gentleman told Alan the matatus to Diani Beach were on the opposite side of the bus terminal, and that Alan should head for the mosque behind it.

Alan struggled through the crowd many of them offered to carry his bag but he ignored everything around him and headed towards the mosque. As he approached the mutatus he heard someone shouting Diani Beach (or something like it). He approached the driver, who spoke fairly good English. Alan wanted to sit in the front seat with his bag and the driver agreed. The driver said that all the passengers at the back were in a group and he expected them to sing hymns all the way. "Sounds good to me," said Alan and with that they made their way out of the madness. With the windows open the singing made the journey more pleasant. They were soon at the Tradewinds Hotel and Alan thanked the people in the back for their good singing. They were so happy they wanted to sing him a special song, but the driver wanted to get on and so he only heard his 'special song' in the distance as they drove away.

Alan checked into the hotel and was shown to his room; it was clean with a double bed, air conditioning and mosquito netting if needed and there was also insect spray. Alan collapsed on the bed and had a little nap. When he awoke, he was not hungry but needed a drink, so he went to the restaurant. For a light meal they had sandwiches but no ostrich meat only lamb, pork or goat. He had eaten goat in Khartoum and chose that, with the compulsory Tusker. After his evening snack he decided to take his second Tusker onto the veranda. He had used insect repellent and was hopeful nothing would bite him. The waiter advised that they regularly sprayed around the hotel, and near the sea there were fewer mosquitoes.

It was a moonlit night and sitting facing the sea with the sound of small waves on the beach was so relaxing; after Khartoum this was close to paradise. He almost forgot his beer, which was getting warmer, but he had decided to drink this one slowly anyway. The peace was disturbed by a group of young people descending on the veranda. They were seated at the next table and Alan detected several English accents. He spoke to one of them who invited him to join their table. Alan pushed his chair and seated himself next to a good-looking lady who looked a bit older than the others. They were backpackers staying at a lodge on the other side of the main road, and they all gave their names, not one remembered by Alan except the lady sitting next to him. Her name was Gwen. He told them he was from Khartoum, worked at the university and was here on holiday. That provoked a bit of discussion then the rest started talking about other things, all except Gwen. She wanted to know more about Khartoum. Actually, Alan did not know all that much about Khartoum as he had never really explored the city. He refrained from telling her about Juba but did a good job describing the university.

At this point most of her companions decided to try another hotel which they had heard was full of Germans. Gwen said she would stay with Alan and they should collect her when they came back. Alan was delighted and, when they had left, she explained she needed to be with someone more her age, but needed them to get back to the lodge. Alan's thoughts were along the lines of I am at least five to ten years older than Gwen but who cares. She explained she had been in Tanzania and had crossed the border two days ago with some of her backpacker companions. She was a nurse and had decided to take a year off. In her family history there was talk of a great grandfather from South Africa. She had visited South Africa before the end of apartheid but was not keen on the social set-up and she being slightly dark skinned felt she was being watched. She had then gone to Tanzania where she was viewed as white and found that easier. Alan had noticed she was well tanned but thought nothing of it. He had not had female company for a while and was enjoying the experience.

They chatted for ages and then the crowd reappeared. Gwen said she would like to come the next day and relax by the sea. Alan was delighted and said he had not planned to go anywhere and that she was truly welcome. When they left Alan was in a bit of a daze; here was an attractive woman who he had just met and he was totally at ease with her. He could not wait for tomorrow to come. As he sat contemplating the next day one of the 'night eagles' approached and asked if he needed more company now his girlfriend had left. He tried to explain she was not his girlfriend but said that he did not need company or the services that might be offered. This seemed to go over the woman's head, but she left him alone. He retired to his room but had trouble sleeping as all he could think about was Gwen. He imagined he could smell her next to him.

Next day they met and spent most of the morning lying on loungers in the shade, chatting. She was from Birmingham and he from Gloucester; she had a couple of younger brothers and he had two elder sisters. Alan had never really discussed his family before, but he was totally relaxed with Gwen and could talk about anything. She wanted to pay for lunch, but he insisted, and they shared fish and chips. In the afternoon again they relaxed and had a dip in the sea. The water was quite warm but neither of them wanted to get out of their depth. Alan had grabbed her as one big wave had threatened to sweep them off their feet; the feel of her body against him was something special.

Alan said he intended to go into Mombasa the next day and asked would Gwen like to join him. She accepted straight away saying she had not yet seen Mombasa. Alan could not believe his luck.

Early next morning they met at the hotel entrance and then hailed a passing matatu. The vehicle was almost empty, so they sat with the driver. He explained that he would probably pick up passengers along the way, but that they would make good time to Mombasa.

Alan decided not to tell the driver they were not in a hurry as that might confuse him as 'all foreigners were in a hurry'. The journey was quite pleasant but there was no choir in the back. Alan had consulted his map and the bus terminal was not far from the centre of town. As soon as they exited the terminal, the chaos subsided and they could stroll casually towards the centre of town.

Alan had told Gwen about the Carnivore and she was keen to go there. Alan thought the best thing to do was to enter one of the Indian owned shops and ask the directions to the Carnivore. They passed several shops and Alan noticed there were very few with large guards outside except one or two jewellery stores. Gwen seemed to be interested in the textile shops but when Alan offered to take her inside, she declined. Finally, they came upon a shop with a microscope in the window; it also had the normal souvenir items, but the microscope attracted Alan's attention. This shop was crowded with all sorts of odd items and of course the Indian owner was keen to talk about his merchandise. Alan was fascinated by several items: a leather box with UV/visible light cuvettes and some glass prisms. Gwen looked on with interest when Alan started to explain some of them should be in a university science lab. Alan asked the owner where he had bought them. The owner explained that the customs would sometimes have auctions of unclaimed items and he had bought them as a job lot. The owner showed Alan a "funny" light pen. Now Alan got excited but tried not to show it. This was a laser pointer, like one he had seen at a conference before he came to Sudan. Alan was not a good haggler, but he had learned a bit in Khartoum. The owner said Alan could have them at a good price as he needed the space for other goods. Alan said he had no room in his suitcase and anyway what would he do with them. Gwen was silently watching this banter and was enjoying the contest. The owner offered his lowest price, which he claimed would mean he would not make a profit and as Alan was getting tired of the combat he accepted. After paying Alan almost forgot to ask for directions.

As they left the shop, Gwen asked why he had bought those items; she could see that Alan was grinning from ear to ear. "Well they will all be donated to the university, the cuvettes will go to the chemistry department and I will use the prisms and laser pointer. I have lectured on lasers and now I can demonstrate them." Gwen could see the passion he had for his job and she liked what she saw. She saw how he gripped his bag of goodies and how happy he was. She might have bought a few carvings or trinkets, but she could see how more valuable to Alan were the things he had bought.

They reached the Carnivore restaurant a little before lunch time. On entering the place, Alan saw it had a similar décor to the one in Nairobi. Alan was in a jovial mood and said if Gwen was game, she should try an ostrich sandwich and he would try the crocodile sandwich. If she was hungry or if she did not like her sandwich, she should order anything she desired. She declined and said they should share the sandwiches. Alan thought this lady must be reading his mind as he wanted to see if the ostrich sandwich was as good as the one in Nairobi. They were both pleased with their respective sandwiches and ordered another ostrich sandwich with, of course, a second Tusker beer each.

They wandered out of the air-conditioned restaurant into a humid, hot Mombasa. Alan was much more affected by the heat than Gwen. He started to tell her about the dry heat in Khartoum and that he preferred it. As they walked, Alan admitted that Mombasa had a lot more to offer than Khartoum but to live here he might need a change of clothes more than twice a day. Gwen was inwardly laughing at Alan's small talk, but she was itching to see Khartoum. They wandered around for a while seeing some of the sights but finally, they agreed they both wanted to get back to Diani Beach and so they headed for the bus station. This time Alan had to negotiate with several drivers before they found a matutu where they could both sit in the front seat with the driver.

Back in his room, Alan looked with interest at his new possessions, but realized he should have asked Gwen to sleep with him. She had sat next to him in the matutu and not recoiled from his touch but would he have got his suggestion right? He was afraid she would say no and end the best time he had ever had. Was it the time, was it the place? She was younger than him, but did that matter? All these thoughts were going through his brain, so he decided to go to the bar and relax. At the bar was a man who was obviously English, and they got talking. This man had arrived in 1950 to join the police force. After independence he had stayed on and taken Kenyan citizenship. He had a Kenyan wife and a house about a kilometre from the hotel. He used the hotel like a local pub as the bar was generally friendly. Alan was slightly amused at the number of people who seemed to tell him their life story without any prodding on his behalf. They chatted for a while and, as Alan was about to leave, he was approached by one of the local ladies but he declined her invitation; there was only Gwen on his mind.

The next morning Gwen joined him on the beach and apologized for not seeing him the previous evening. She had gone to her room, laid down, and slept one of the best sleeps she had experienced on her travels. She had enjoyed the trip to Mombasa and was surprised how tired it had made her. Alan was thinking this was something, when a woman was apologizing to him for falling asleep; she was special. As the days passed, he had not slept with her, but she was his constant companion and he was dreading their parting. She said she would try to get to Khartoum after seeing a bit more of Kenya and Ethiopia. He told her about the Sudan Club and that if she got to Khartoum he could be contacted there. He was regretting not trying to sleep with her, but he had tried not to spoil a great relationship.

The day he left Gwen had said goodbye and given him a kiss and he wished he could take her with him; for him it was an unhappy parting. A matutu to Mombasa, a taxi to the airport and his journey to Kenya was almost over. There were still a couple of surprises. He found that he was required to change his Kenyan shillings into foreign currency which he did. At the airline desk he found out that he had to pay a departure tax in Kenyan shillings, so went back to the exchange to lose more money.

On returning to Khartoum he found the university open and lectures resumed. He used his laser pen and the prisms and Kenya started to fade in his memory. What did not fade was Gwen. At night he lay on his bed and thought of her. Where was she, and would she meet someone her own age? After a couple of weeks, he was back into his old routine. The weather was getting a little cooler and he much preferred it to the humidity of Mombasa. One afternoon as he entered the Sudan Club, the guard said he had a guest. As he approached the mustaba his pulse started to race; that outline was Gwen. He recognized her even though she had her back to him. He had to stop and breathe deeply to contain his emotions; she had come to Khartoum to see him!

Gwen greeted him with a kiss and said how wonderful and serene the Sudan Club was. He sat down beside her and asked if she would like a drink. She said she had tried a soft drink but it was too sweet for her. "You must try a fruit juice; they know how to do it for me so I will order two." She agreed this was a better drink. He asked where she was staying, and her reply was that she would like to stay with him in his apartment. Now he was in raptures and stuttered, "Certainly, yes, yes, yes." On reflection he sounded needy, but it was done and it was honest. For their evening meal they had the 'compulsory' fish and chips.

On the drive to his place he told her it might be a bit messy as the house girl who cleaned the flat had gone missing. He explained it was on the third floor and had never seen a mosquito and while they had electricity, they had water. A power cut would mean the top tank would soon be empty. He was thinking to himself, why am I saying all this trivia? As they entered his street, he pointed out the four-storey building in a sea of one- and two-storey houses. Her luggage was a well packed backpack and he persuaded her that he would carry it up the stairs. The flat had minimal furniture mostly made of packing case wood. There was a double rope bed called an angreeb and also a single bed in the living room. On the balcony there were two recliner chairs and a small barbecue. They sat on those chairs with Alan's home-made fruit juice which was nice and cold. Gwen loved the view from the balcony and could not wait to see it in daylight.

When it was time for bed Alan offered to sleep on the small bed in the living room and Gwen could have the double bed. "Why not sleep with me there is plenty of room in the double bed," she replied.

Alan gasped he could not believe his ears. She said "Don't worry. I am on the pill." Gwen admitted she had wanted to sleep with him in Kenya, but there were too many eyes and ears and people would start gossiping. Alan admitted that he had wanted to ask her but was afraid of a rejection that would mean the loss of a dear friend. That night was a dream come true for both of them. Alan was gentle and, if anything, Gwen was more dominant but they both experienced a climax and fell asleep in each other's arms.

When Alan awoke, he could not believe his luck but he had things to do. Alan apologized for having to go to work, he had two lectures in the morning and then after lunch he had two more lectures, and he might not be able to make it for lunch due to the traffic. There was not much in the fridge as he only went to the market early in the morning. Little fresh food would be available in the market when he finished in the afternoon. There were eggs, local bread some local tomatoes and potatoes but no meat. There was some fruit but not much, and she was welcome to anything she could eat. He was feeling a bit bad, but she said she would be OK and she had some washing to do and not to worry about her.

His lectures were bit disorganized as all he could think of was Gwen. At lunch he met a friend and had to tell him some of the story. His friend reminded him that they lived under Sharia and if he was stopped by the police, he should call her ochti (sister) and if the policeman were more educated to explain she was his sister-in-law and while she was visiting Sudan, he was her guardian. Alan had not thought much about Sharia in respect to their relationship but thanked his friend for the advice, which luckily was never needed.

Arriving back to the flat he found her sitting on the balcony admiring the view. The flat was clean and everything in order and she said she had enjoyed a nice peaceful day. Alan promised that he only had one tutorial the next day and they could go shopping in the morning, then he would take her to the Sudan Club and join her after his tutorial. She agreed to anything he had planned. He said they should go to eat at the Syrian club as they had some of the tastiest food in town and one barbecued chicken dish he had tried, was particularly delicious. The Syrian club was livelier than the Sudan Club and the food was excellent. On the drive home Alan realized he had some condoms. A lady had come to Sudan to distribute condoms but had found the locals unreceptive and so had gone off to Uganda. She had given him some samples but he had not used them. He had second thoughts about mentioning this to Gwen and so said nothing.

Shopping in the market the next day was a revelation. Gwen was much better at haggling than Alan and he reckoned he saved nearly fifty percent on his bill. At the Sudan Club he bought Gwen a temporary membership for two weeks; the manager was very pleased as revenue was down since the imposition of Sharia. He explained to the manager, that she was his sister-in-law. After lunch he went to his tutorial and Gwen relaxed by the pool. When he came back to the club she wanted to go and cook dinner in his flat. He agreed but said they should at least have an alcoholic drink to celebrate their first home-cooked dinner. He left her in the flat while he went out searching for a bottle. There was a place where he bought tarmia and they knew him as he often bought one of his favourite snacks. He knew somewhere nearby there was grog and they would 'find' it for him if he asked. The only thing available was Aragi, the Ethiopian brandy he preferred was in short supply.

The tarmia were added to her dinner and Gwen loved them. He warned her not to drink too much Aragi as he was not sure of its quality. This was a meal to remember, she had beaten the meat and barbecued it, she had cooked the potatoes, sliced them and barbecued them and boiled the broad beans with some spices. The Syrian club with its barbecued meat had influenced her cooking. Alan never had a home-cooked meal like this and he said so. In the next two weeks they ate fewer meals at the club and more in his flat.

It had to happen; one evening they had a power cut and that reduced their nocturnal enjoyment (just too hot for vigorous sex) but they sat out on the balcony enjoying each other's company and the peace and quiet a power cut brings. It was nearing the time when Gwen would leave. She said that she would like to live in Khartoum with Alan but Sharia was an impediment.

"It would not be an impediment if you married me," said Alan.

"I was hoping you would say that. Are you proposing marriage?"

"You bet I am. You are the best thing in my life"

"I accept."

During the next few days, they planned the wedding; it would be in a registry office in Birmingham between Boxing Day and New Year when Alan had leave. They would have a small reception in a hotel, preferably where his parents would be staying. Alan was so excited he wanted to phone his parents, but the phone system had gone downhill so far, he had to write letters. The letters to his parents and two sisters were all similar with a few details of his meeting with Gwen in Kenya and their reconnection in Khartoum. The replies came and his eldest sister was enthusiastic, his mother's letter was full of questions and his second sister had lots of reservations. These letters arrived well after Gwen had left and there were probably no questions that he could not answer himself.

His eldest sister was married with two children and lived near Birmingham, in Stourbridge. She was always positive and had often told Alan to look for a wife; she took after their father. Alan's second sister was a very cautious person and wanted to weigh up every angle before making a decision; she took after their mother. His mother's letter was all about the length of time he had known Gwen; she knew nothing of the intensity of his feelings. He wondered whether his father had seen the reply or even his original letter. He really wanted to talk to his father but that would have to wait till he arrived in England.

Gwen had made all the arrangements and her family were very happy with them. Alan could hardly wait for his leave; he even started telling some of his students he was getting married. He had to conduct some exams before Christmas and he found he was being too generous in his marking — the happiness factor.

Arriving in England he hired a car and drove straight to see Gwen before going to Gloucester. She was so happy to see him and introduced him to her parents and brothers. He was at ease in this company and they all wanted to know about Sudan and his job. He decided to stop at his sister's house on the way to Gloucester and Gwen went with him. Alan's eldest sister Molly was most welcoming, and she and Gwen hit it off straight away, Molly had trained to be a nurse before marriage and so they had a lot in common. Molly drove Gwen home and Alan proceeded on his way.

As Alan drove down the M5 to Gloucester he was glad he had taken Gwen to see Molly. He was now heading home and a bit worried about how he was going to handle the next few hours. Arriving home, he realized there was a potentially hostile environment and so he asked his father to go to the pub as he was longing for a beer. His mother seemed a bit miffed, but he told her about Sharia and she seemed to understand. In the pub he found that his father had not seen the reply letters from his mother or from Angela, his second sister. Alan was most insistent that this was going to be a good marriage and Molly was on his side. His father laughed and said his mother would come around she was just being protective, but he was not so sure about Angela. The local beer was good, but Alan thought he preferred Tusker.

The Christmas period was a bit disjointed. Alan spent Christmas Eve introducing Gwen to his parents Christmas Day, he spent with his parents and Boxing Day with Gwen's family. On Christmas Eve he picked up Gwen in the morning and took her for lunch at his parents' home. The initial greetings were cordial but then Angela started asking about Gwen's background. Gwen explained she had worked as a nurse in a hospital in Birmingham and had met many patients but one in particular had impressed her. He was from South Africa and had lived under apartheid but was not bitter; he missed his homeland. He said Gwen should go and visit for him and tell him her impression when she got back. Gwen did not say one of her ancestors was South African. She decided to take time off and visit Africa. The bad part was that when she got back, the man was dead. She had placed a wreath on his grave. That broke

Angela's resistance and Alan felt his mother was softening. Alan's dad whispered, "I like this girl."

As Alan drove Gwen back to Birmingham, she told him she had Angela coming around, but his mother was a bit difficult. Alan thought she had got it completely right; he might have to work on his mother a bit more, but dad was on side. Christmas Day was spent with his parents and he tried to field all the questions his mother bought forth. The next day he had a much more pleasant Boxing Day and stayed the night with Gwen, a great Christmas present.

The wedding was two days later, and his parents and Angela stayed at a hotel on the Hagley Road. Angela invited a man Alan had not met, but he seemed a decent bloke. The wedding and reception went well, and it looked like his mother was resigned to the situation. Alan and Gwen stayed in the same hotel and in the morning they all had a very pleasant breakfast. His father was in a very jovial mood and started to dominate the conversation. Alan had never seen him do that before. Alan and Gwen had a short honeymoon in London, but the prime objective was to start the visa process for Gwen. Not long after New Year, which they spent in London enjoying the fireworks, Alan had to leave for Sudan.

Within a couple of weeks Gwen joined Alan in Khartoum and was glad to be in the warm sun. Winter in Khartoum was the best, the temperature only occasionally went above thirty degrees centigrade, and the dryness made this very pleasant. She soon found a job in Abdu's uncle's hospital and they enjoyed the next year of togetherness. Towards the end of the year Alan got a warning that the UK government were no longer supporting science in Sudan so he should look for another job.

They were sad to leave Sudan and all the friends they had made. Going back to the UK in the summer could prepare them for the anticipated cold winter. Alan got a job in a technical college in Shropshire and Gwen got a job in a local hospital.

After more than twenty years of marriage they still adore each other. Bedroom sex is a must and regular. They unfortunately have no children but have a very busy social life, and stories of Khartoum can still fascinate their friends. When Alan meets new people, he tells them he only went to Kenya once and found Tusker, the beer he was looking for, but he also found a wife and she was the best find of his life.

Sharia

William, everyone called him Bill from a tender age, came to Khartoum in October 1983, just after the imposition of Sharia law. He did not know how that law would have a great effect on his life. He knew nothing about the law and was unaware that Sharia had recently been imposed on the whole of Sudan. President Nimeri had declared that all alcoholic drinks would be destroyed and thrown into the Nile; if only Bill had known.

Bill had fixed up a job in Africa at an interview in London two months earlier. A pleasant man with fuzzy hair in a pale blue suit had interviewed him in a cheap hotel in Bayswater. What had impressed Bill was the colour of the man's skin, almost jet black. The pale blue suit and the colour of the man's skin had fixed an image in Bill's mind he found hard to erase. Except for a few details the interview had been easy, relaxing and forgettable. The man asked about Bill's background and work experience (which Bill exaggerated) in perfect English. After the interview they went to a nearby pub and Bill noticed the man only drank orange juice. Later Bill found out that he was not his employer but a professional interviewer with many contacts with small companies in the Sudan; being a strict Muslim he did not touch alcohol.

Within a few days he received a job offer and a request for his passport so that a visa could be obtained from the Sudanese Embassy. The salary was quoted in Sudanese pounds and looked impressive and with two months annual leave and paid return airfare Bill was over the moon. He called his girlfriend, Angela, and told her the good news; she seemed less enthusiastic about his imminent departure. That evening they went to a local pub to celebrate, Bill in an elated mood and Angela in a gloomy one. She seemed to be trying to put a damper on the evening by asking questions. What did he know about the Sudan? How much of this salary would trickle back to the UK? Bill shrugged off the questions as he did not have any answers and proceeded to get very drunk, telling everyone in the pub about his fabulous new job. Many people had similar questions to Angela but he gave glib, flippant answers satisfying himself but not the questioner. No one was going to stop his enjoyment. As the night wore on Bill got louder and more exaggerated in his answers to questions. Angela was getting more and more embarrassed and was urging him to leave. Finally, she stood up, emptied her glass and left the pub as fast as she could.

Bill sat in a daze for a few seconds and then realized he was free to roam about the pub telling everyone his good fortune. Maybe Angela had her period, he thought to himself. That was his last thought of Angela that evening as he became too busy boring everyone in the pub who would listen to him. As the night wore on, he became more and more drunk and loud, until finally the barman refused to serve him. Bill had great difficulty in finding his way to the exit and then more difficulty opening the door and propelling himself into the street. He sat on the steps and realized how drunk he was and was glad he had not driven to the pub on his prized possession, his Triumph 500. As he staggered home, he realised how tired he was, but he had enjoyed his night out.

At seven a.m. his alarm went off and to Bill this was an explosion in his brain. Oh, the pain! He had to move to stop the bloody thing ringing and he realized he was fully clothed. Flopping back on the bed he was feeling dizzy and sick; he was still drunk. In a matter of minutes, he was asleep and did not wake till eleven a.m. He was very thirsty, but he could now stand without swaying and feeling sick. What a night he had had in the pub. How had he got home? After a few glasses of water, he felt sick again and flopped on the bed. Little did he know that drinking water was to become a big part of his life. He could no longer get back to sleep and Angela kept drifting in and out of his thoughts. She was obviously in a bad mood and Bill could not think of anything he had done to upset her. He would give her time to apologize and she would come around in a couple of days.

By the time he finally left his bed it was midday and he was feeling much better. He called in sick at work and then looked for his passport. The passport was almost brand new only having been used to go to Portugal; now he was going to go to Africa. The sounds of the words Africa and Sudan pleased him, and he said them over and over putting stress on *Africa, Sudan, Africa, Sudan.*

After a couple of days Bill returned to work, most of the time at home he had spent daydreaming of Africa or sleeping. He had been to the library to consult atlases and find books on the Sudan. The public library had few useful books specifically on the Sudan so he settled on books of Africa. He did not read most of the books, only looking at the pictures. Bill had done very little reading since leaving technical college with a Higher National Certificate in Mechanical Engineering. Bill actually did very little except sleep, work and occasionally get drunk.

The boss was not very happy when Bill gave his notice about one hour after resuming work, but on reflection he was not too bothered that Bill was leaving. Bill was not a good consistent worker and finding a replacement should not be hard. On further reflection the boss decided that Bill's job could be phased out, saving the company money. Bill was never a hard worker but in the last two weeks his output had hit an all-time low. He spent most of his time wandering around the factory boring everyone with his fabulous new job. Most of the rest of the time he daydreamed about perpetual sunshine, swimming pools, palm trees and the desert. Life was all going to be so good. On the day of his leaving some of the workers took him to the pub for lunch, most of them went along as a matter of tradition rather than through desire. Bill had succeeded in boring or alienating all of them in the last two weeks.

Two problems arose in those two weeks: one was Angela, the second was no reply from London about his visa. Bill waited a few days for Angela to call and apologize but she had not done so. Finally, he had called her at work and she had sounded very unenthusiastic about meeting him, but she had finally agreed that could meet, anywhere except a pub. They went for a ride and stopped at a roadside café. The conversation had been difficult, and Bill had been warned not to talk about the night in the pub. They went home early and when he dropped Angela at her flat, he had expected to be invited in for a coffee, but all she would allow was a peck on the cheek. Bill went to the nearest pub to collect his thoughts. Why was she being unreasonable? Could she be jealous of his opportunity or maybe she thought he would pick up some African bird in the Sudan. He could not see that his behaviour was any reason for her coolness. After a few pints he came to the conclusion that she must love him and would come around in time. He made up his mind that when he was settled, he would send for her. A few days later they took a ride to the same café (he could not think of anywhere else to go).

This evening had been a little friendlier as he had not talked too much about Africa, but at the end he had only received a peck on the cheek. Again, he rationalized it over a few pints in the pub that she would soon come around.

There was still no word on his visa after ten days. He had phoned the number on the letterhead that had offered him the job but all he could get was an answering machine. He had left several urgent messages but had no reply. After a few days a letter arrived apologising for the delay and any future delays. The problem was the Sudanese Embassy, they were always slow in processing visas. The Sudanese Embassy, although a little slow, rarely took more than a week over a visitor's visa with no complications. What Bill did not know was that the interviewer was awaiting a reply from Khartoum and Bill's passport had not even been submitted to the embassy. These were difficult times in Khartoum and Bill was unaware of the situation.

Now he had no job, and only two weeks money and a small amount of holiday pay. Notice had been given on his flat and there was one week to go. What if there were further delays? The question started to bother him. Although not on speaking terms with his parents he had written them a letter informing them of his good fortune. If the worst came to the worst, he could always stay with them. He dreaded the thought as after a couple of days grace there would be continuous arguments with his mother or father, or both. They would nag him about his drinking or untidiness or his general lifestyle. He prayed that his passport would arrive before he had to go and live at home.

Angela was no help during this period; she was cool towards him and full of little criticisms. He wanted to tell her to shut up when she was critical but was afraid to do so as she was the only one he could talk to. She might refuse to see him if he was rude to her. Again, he phoned London and left a message on the infernal answering machine. He gave his parents address which would be the place for any communication after the end of the week. No answer came and so he said goodbye to Angela on Friday and drove to his parents' home. He left some clothes and his stereo with Angela and said he would pick them up in a week's time.

The weekend was pleasant with his parents; they seemed pleased he had a new job. He went with his dad to the pub on Sunday lunch time and his dad recounted some of his experiences in Egypt during the war. Bill's dad had been in the Eighth Army and had spent most of his time in Egypt and Libya. Bill was able to tell his dad about the frustration of the visa process and his dad understood, telling Bill that African time was different to UK time; it was more relaxed. His dad was very different from their last meeting; he was a little critical of Bill giving up his job so soon but was glad Bill could spend some time with them. Actually, that was the last thing Bill wanted to do, but he had to make the best of his stay. His mother was full of fantasies about Africa, she was an avid watcher of wild life TV programmes. During the days, his father was consulting atlases and telling stories about Cairo. He had been in the desert during the summer and it was 'bloody hot' and Bill should drink large amounts of fluids. Bill was not good at taking advice but plenty of beer sounded good.

During the following week, his passport and airline tickets arrived redirected from his old address, the only problem was that the flight was not for a couple of weeks. His parents were delighted, and his father reminded Bill that he would have to adjust to African time. Bill called Angela and told her the good news, but she did not sound too enthusiastic. After several phone calls he had found a shipping agent who would send his motorbike to Port Sudan. He delivered the bike to Liverpool with photocopies of all his papers. The trip to Liverpool was a good break from his parents but his money was disappearing fast.

At last he was on the way. He had visited Angela a couple of times and she seemed to be warming to his leaving but otherwise was very cold towards him. He could not wait to get set up in Khartoum and then he would send for her; he would keep her! His parents had been very good; he could hardly believe it. His mother had tears in her eyes when he left, and his father had given him the money to ship his bike to the Sudan. His father advised that when he got to Khartoum he should ask for 'transport money' and when he had his bike, they could reimburse him. His father kept saying how he wished he was going and maybe when he settled, they would come for a holiday. Bill was not too enthusiastic about that idea but he kept his thoughts to himself.

Arriving in London on a wet Friday afternoon Bill could only think about sunshine and lots of Sudanese pounds. He was almost broke and he felt insecure but really looking forward to a bright future. The interviewer a fuzzy haired man had booked him into a hotel in Paddington where he would spend the night. He was going to be taken out to dinner so he would not have to spend the few pounds he had. A car would pick him up on Saturday morning and take him to the airport. He was feeling good but his well-being was dented a little when he arrived at the hotel. It was very run down and looked grimy, the decorations seemed to be Victorian or older. The place was dark and his room was no better. He could put up with this dismal place though, as he was only staying one night.

Dining out was more pleasant, they had a good meal in an Indian restaurant where his host seemed to be well known. Bill was well fed with food and beer and was feeling good. His host was called Abdul and he talked in glowing terms about Khartoum and some place called Kassala. He talked at length about the Nile, the desert and the weather. The Nile was the life blood of the Sudan, "No Nile, no Sudan," he kept saying. "Khartoum is the meeting place of three Niles: the White, the Blue and the River Nile". Bill got the impression that Abdul really missed Sudan and on a rainy London day who could not understand his homesickness. Abdul explained that the weather might be a little warm at first, but in late November it would cool down and it would be a surprise if it rained. Bill was almost drooling at the thought of perpetual sunshine. "You may not see rain until June or July," he was told. Bill was as intoxicated by the talk as the beer. As they were about to leave the restaurant Abdul gave Bill a couple of packages and a few letters that Bill was to give to the man who would meet him at the airport and help Bill through immigration and customs. They parted with a handshake and Abdul saying, "I will see you next in *our* capital."

Heathrow had a few surprises for Bill the next day. The first came when he tried to change a ten-pound note into Sudanese pounds. "Sorry, that is a restricted currency," was the reply from the teller. Bill did not understand the term 'restricted currency' and wanted to ask a few questions but there was a queue behind him so he put his note back in his pocket and wandered over to the Sudan Airways desk.

As he approached the Sudan Airways area the density of the crowd grew and the amount of luggage was astonishing. No one seemed to be queuing and so he approached the desk. He heard the girl behind the desk call out, "Is there anyone without excess luggage ready to check in?" Bill gingerly approached the desk and all eyes seemed to be on him. "Thank goodness.

You are the first person to check in; everyone else seems to be travelling with everything but the kitchen sink. Whenever this airline flies there is a problem with luggage, but at least they are a quiet bunch not like the Nigerians. I've refused to work on the Nigerian Airways desk." Bill looked back at the crowd behind him and they were all smiling.

The next surprise came at the duty-free shop, where he produced his ticket as he was about to pay for a bottle of whisky and was told, "Sorry luv, they won't let booze onto their aircraft or into their country."

"Since when and why?" asked Bill.

"Sometime last month, sorry luv." Then to cap it all the plane was delayed. To hell with it thought Bill I need a drink. After an expensive couple of pints of beer, he was joined at the table by a man he had seen at the Sudan Airways desk. The man started to talk and said that he had noticed Bill was going to Khartoum. Bill asked him about the country 'going dry.' The Sudanese admitted that he did not know too much as he had spent the last few months in the UK, but he had been told that President Numeri had declared that Sharia law was to be the law of Sudan. Lots of booze had been dumped in the Nile and the joke at the moment was about drunken crocodiles. The Sharia law was supposed to be for the whole country and the man started to chuckle as he repeated, "Whole country!"

Bill asked "What is so funny? I think it is a bad idea." The Sudanese then started to tell Bill he was from the south and that they would never give up their local beer and spirits. Bill interrupted, asking, "Wow will it affect me?"

"Foreigners in the Sudan seem to do as they please; we need them and I can't see any of them staying without booze, even the missionaries drink!"

The man left and Bill decided to have another pint. Just as he took his first sip, they announced that passengers for Sudan Airways should board the plane. Bill decided to finish his beer first; it could be the last for a while. When he finally embarked, he was one of the last passengers and the plane was engulfed in noisy conversations in loud Arabic. Bill observed that there were a few white passengers, but they were scattered around the plane. Bill was seated at the back next to a black couple; he noticed how dark their complexion was like his interviewer; at least he had an aisle seat.

The flight was pretty horrendous. Bill was quite tall and his legs did not fit comfortably in the space provided. Passengers seemed to be in motion the whole flight, and as he was seated near the toilets there was always a line-up near his seat. The man in the middle seat was up and down like yo-yo, talking to friends or queuing for the toilet. The food was inedible: a piece of chicken on cold sticky rice, a square of cheese and biscuits and coffee. The coffee was the only thing he enjoyed. Worst of all there were no alcoholic drinks. There was no liquor on this plane explained one of the stewardesses, as she apologised. On his only visit to the lavatory he did notice one man drinking from a bottle in a paper bag. How had he got it on board? By the time they landed in Khartoum, Bill was tired, in a bad mood and thirsty; he had drunk more water on this flight than he had drunk since he was a child.

The first thing that struck Bill as he came through the plane door to descend the steps was the heat. It was near midnight and it was still hot; it reminded Bill of what his father had said about Cairo. There was a kind of mist that gave all the lights a halo effect and there was a taste to the air; it was fine sand. Bill's eyes started to water, and he could feel sand in his mouth. Looking around Bill thought that it was a poor excuse for an airport; the one at Faro had been smaller but better. As he walked to the terminal building it was though he was walking towards a fire, as the building was radiating heat. The skin beneath his shirt was sweating and he still had his jacket on which made him feel hotter. His brow was dry, though, and his nostrils were even more so. No one had told him it was going to be like this.

Passing into the courtyard in front of the terminal he noticed a small man holding a piece of cardboard with Bill's name on it. The man had a broad smile that seemed to increase as Bill walked towards him. He was pointing rapidly back and forth from Bill to the cardboard. Bill nodded in confirmation and the man started talking in rapid English. Bill only understood about half of what was said and after a few sentences had to butt in to ask questions.

The ubiquitous 'Mr Fixit' was called Ali and he was here to smooth Bill's passage through customs and immigration and then to see him to the hotel. Ali asked his first question in an undertone, "Do you have any booze?" Bill's negative reply seemed to disappoint Ali, but he said, "No problem then." As they entered the terminal building the temperature seemed to climb and now Bill was starting to notice how dry his mouth had become. He could taste the sand and the inside of his mouth felt sticky; his nose was so dry it was almost painful. Bill let his eyes wander around the room. The place needed painting badly; it looked like it had needed paint for a decade or more. The ceiling fans were slowly rotating but no breeze seemed to be coming Bill's way

People were in groups, clustered around tables filling out their immigration and customs forms or queuing at the immigration desk. Ali thrust a form into Bill's hand and said, "Fill this out and give me your passport." Bill did as he was told; he was too tired to ask questions. Ali asked Bill to wait and proceeded to exit through a door opposite to where the officers were checking passports. After a short while Bill caught sight of Ali talking to an officer behind the immigration desk. Ali motioned Bill to come past the immigration desk and so Bill sheepishly strolled past the queue into the customs hall. This hall was incredible; there were people everywhere, baggage everywhere and no luggage carts. Bill thought about the check-in at

Heathrow and was anxious to see how much baggage would arrive. "Where is the baggage?" he asked.

"It will come soon." They stood for a while and nothing happened except more people entered the room. Bill was hot, sticky and tired and longed to get to a bed but first he must drink.

The baggage hall was now packed with people, and they were at least two deep around the 'carousel'. Not exactly a carousel but a short conveyor belt that entered through a hole in the wall and after about twenty feet disappeared through another hole in the wall. Bill propped himself up by a wall even though it seemed warm to the touch. There were no seats and he did not want to sit on the floor. After about an hour (or that is what it seemed like to Bill) the conveyor belt started moving. The noise became louder and people were jumping up and down to see the emerging baggage. At the end of the belt was a porter throwing the unpicked baggage into a pile. The people who could find their baggage on the belt had to struggle through the crowd to get it out. Bill decided that although he was taller than most of the crowd and could force his way to the front, he would hang back until the crowd thinned. All this time Ali seemed unconcerned and had been chatting to some Sudanese around him. Then suddenly the belt jammed and stopped, and Bill saw his suitcase in a pile where the porter had been throwing them. This pile was quite a sight; it contained boxes and bags of all sizes and suitcases of all descriptions. Some of them were so large

Bill could only wonder how one person could carry them. Bill imagined someone dragging a full suitcase of massive size and that seemed to cheer him up a bit.

Having retrieved his bag, he motioned to Ali and they joined the queue for customs inspection. They were opening every bag and this was another very slow process. When Bill finally got to the customs desk, he placed his suitcase on a concrete table, and was asked to open the case. Ali spoke a few words to the customs officer who then asked, "Any liquor or magazines?"

"No," said Bill.

"You can go," said the officer with a big toothy smile after putting a chalk dollar sign on Bill's suitcase. As they pushed their way through the crowd Bill asked Ali why he wanted to know about magazines.

Ali broke into a big grin. "They would confiscate magazines with girls who were not fully clothed. It is against Sharia. Anyway, they have orders to open every bag, but no one gave them orders to see, so they see what they want to see."

Ali found his battered old Toyota in the car park and Bill was aghast at the thought of riding in the old wreck. As he looked around the car park, he saw many like it and so resigned himself to a ride to he knew not where. Surprisingly the car started first time and they manoeuvred their way out of the airport avoiding the pedestrians who seemed oblivious of the moving cars, while avoiding haphazardly parked cars. Bill was feeling really sleepy but the breeze coming through the car window kept him awake, that and Ali's driving.

They finally reached the Hotel Oasis down a dark unpaved and bumpy backstreet. By this time Bill was passed caring what anything looked like; all he wanted to do was drink and sleep. His room was not unpleasant but like everything else needed painting. The only drink available was water but it tasted good and Bill downed several glasses. Ali took his leave and said he would be back in the morning and for Bill to stay in his room until Ali arrived. Bill was glad to be left alone and flopped on the bed fully clothed and promptly fell asleep. Halfway through the night he awoke and decided he should undress and drink the now tepid water and then he fell asleep again.

Bill was awakened by someone knocking on the door. It was Ali, back so soon. Before opening the door, Bill swallowed a couple of glasses of water, his mouth still dry. After he was dressed Ali took him to breakfast. The hotel 'eggs and sausage' were nothing like British ones. The eggs were greasy and the sausages were small and tough. The bread was dry and had a funny taste, the coffee was like sludge and the only good thing was the cold water. Ali talked almost the whole time through breakfast and although Bill was not listening most of the time, he did catch that they were off to see the boss.

In daylight the hotel was depressing and outside was worse. Everything was sandy brown, including the hotel pool which had no water but a layer of sand on the bottom. The drive to work was like entering a different world. The route they took had only one tarmac road and every street was full of piles of dirt and potholes, although at least the potholes were dry. The factory, which turned out to be little more than a large workshop, was in the industrial area. To get there they crossed a tarmacked road bridge and below was a railway marshalling yard full of old locomotives, carriages and trucks, but no movement. Crossing the bridge, they were in a traffic jam and Bill started to feel the heat and it was only eight a.m. The cars, trucks and buses seemed to be mostly old and battered but at least some of the trucks were brightly painted. The buses were full to overloading and people were hanging off the doors. Even so, when the buses stopped, they seemed to squeeze on a few more passengers.

They finally reached the industrial estate and the shacks were unbelievable; most were made out of corrugated iron and made the factory where he would work look like a palace. The boss, Wahib, was a little fat man with a much lighter skin colour than Ali. Wahib was a Christian, a Copt. Wahib explained that Bill would be in charge of the workshop which made machine parts to order. Since the imposition of Sharia everything had slowed down and Wahib was going to be busy trying to get new orders. The Sudanese pound had been devalued since Bill had received his appointment letter and in fact unless business picked up Bill could be out of a job. Wahib said that Christians felt threatened by the new law, but he was confident things would settle down. Wahib's frankness took Bill by surprise and of course the biggest surprise was the sudden shrinkage of his salary. Bill did not even ask for a transport allowance and Wahib intimated that Bill would be 'carried' to and from work. Bill did drop the hint that he had very little money and had not been able to change the few pounds he had. Wahib expressed surprise that Ali had not tried to change some pounds as foreign currency was big on the black market especially the US dollar and the UK pound. Wahib gave Bill fifty Sudanese pounds and let him have the day off.

Wahib had instructed the driver to take Bill to the hotel or to the Sudan Club if Bill wished to go there. Wahib told Bill the Sudan Club was the British club and had a restaurant and a bar. The word bar excited Bill. Wahib said that one of his cousins was married to a British lady and was a member of the club. Bill was soon to find that brother, sister or cousin had a much looser meaning in Sudan than in the UK, although being a Copt, Wahib's use of the word cousin could have been accurate in the British sense too.

The Sudan Club was a bit of an anti-climax; on the gate was a forbidding notice saying 'Members Only' and the gate boy informed him that he would have to get a member to sign him in but that he could talk to the manager. The manager was an unsmiling young Copt who gave Bill a membership application that had to be signed by two members. (The application fee looked enormous, and he would also have to produce his British passport.) As there were not many members in the club the manager said he would not have to be signed in on this day. The manager warned that he could only come to the club three times before he had to become a member. The restaurant was open, but the bar only sold soft drinks; the booze was locked in the store until it had been determined whether foreigners would be allowed to drink.

The best part of the Sudan Club was the garden, with the swimming pool, and the difference to the scene outside the gate was unbelievable. Outside it was dusty brown, chaos and noise all around, everything needed a paint job and lots of repairs, particularly the pavements. Inside the club it was clean, quiet and peaceful; there were mown lawns, flowers, clean trees and a sparkling-blue swimming pool. Even the buildings looked as though they had recently been painted white. Bill did not normally notice these things, but the sheer contrast made it hard not to. Bill sat by the pool and realized he should go to the hotel to get his bathing costume. As he left the club, he told the gate boy, "I will be back." He found the driver and went back to the hotel. Back at the club he enjoyed swimming and the best couple of hours in Khartoum.

At lunch time some members came to the Club and Bill was able to chat to a few of them. They all lamented the booze being locked up but most thought that they would be allowed to drink soon. For lunch Bill had the staple dish 'fish and chips' the only thing different from home was that the fish was 'twisted', but he enjoyed it. One member was quite friendly, and they chatted all afternoon. Bill found out that since the law change very few members came to the club. As his friend put it, they went home to their dwindling stocks. This new-found friend was called John and he had been a member for several years; he did not drink much so Sharia had affected him little, but most of the other expats were heavy drinkers and they seemed to be in a state of shock. There was illegal stuff around, but the real liquor was expensive and the cheaper stuff was of dubious quality. Most people were afraid of getting caught as to do so could get you twenty-five lashes for being drunk, or even smelling of alcohol, plus a night in terrible police cells. During their discussion, the gate boy came with a message from the driver that he wanted to go home; John said he would drop Bill at the Oasis Hotel so that solved the problem.

The next few weeks were hell for Bill; he had moved from the hotel to a dirty sparsely furnished flat in a poor area but within walking distance of his work. There were no expats in the area and his 'transport' had stopped; how he longed to have his bike. He had joined the Sudan Club on a temporary basis as the yearly fees were too large. His salary covered his food, taxi rides and some black-market booze called Aragi, but there was little left that he could send back to the UK. Sending money out of Sudan was very difficult; the only way for

Bill was to buy dollars or pounds on the black market and they were expensive. His job was difficult and often he had to ask advice of the foreman who was helpful and friendly. Wahib was out most of the time getting work and he was having enough success to keep the factory busy. Bill had written to Angela giving her the Sudan Club address but as yet had received no reply.

After a few weeks he had word of his bike which had landed in Port Sudan and was being cleared through customs by one of Wahib's friends. Bill had been dreaming about his bike; that and Angela were all he had in his thoughts. Bill could not be spared from work to pick up the bike so he would have to wait for his prized possession to be delivered by lorry. Finally, the bike arrived in Khartoum, on the back of a battered truck. There were dents and scratches, the head light glass was cracked and one of the footrests was bent. Bill was angry about that but excited and oblivious to the crowd that had gathered to look at this bike which was unique in Khartoum. There were plenty of Japanese bikes and the military had a few old BSAs, but no one had seen a bike like this. Bill took the bike into the workshop and started cleaning it, all thought of work forgotten. No one else was allowed to touch his prized possession; the foreman had suggested one of the workers could clean it but that was immediately rejected. Wahib arrived to find his expert cleaning a motorbike but he understood. The paperwork was shown to Bill and Wahib said the duty and processing could be paid later, this was all forgotten by Bill, he was too absorbed in his 'love'. Wahib did get through that the bike should be registered and insured so that Bill could get 'benzine' coupons. Bill had seen long queues at garages but it had not occurred to him that he would have to get coupons and petrol would be rationed. Wahib had often complained that he had coupons for ten gallons per week but could only get eight and for those he had to queue from dawn. Motorbikes were better off in that they were often allowed to the front of the queue for a gallon.

The next few weeks Bill was having a great time riding all over Khartoum and Omdurman. He found he could get extra petrol on the black market and could go quite far. The battlefield outside Omdurman (where Kitchener had fought the Mahdi) was a prohibited zone but he did get out into the desert and he found the area along the River Nile very interesting. At night he stored his bike under the stairs of his apartment building and while at work he had it inside the factory. Wahib had advised that he immobilize the vehicle whenever he left it in the street, such as near the Sudan Club. Khartoum was starting to be a more interesting place and he was meeting more expats although none of them lived near him.

Parties were generally held on a Thursday as Friday was the day off. One of his new-found friends (he worked for a British Company) was holding a party at a three-bedroomed house in one of the better parts of

Khartoum. Although a bachelor he had servants, a car and a driver. Bill envied him but he was generous and had befriended Bill. The party was going well but the booze was running low, so Bill was sent out to get some more bottles. Bill knew where to get illicit booze and so he gladly went out and came back with a few party savers. The party went on till well after midnight and Bill was one of the last to leave at four a.m. Exiting the garden Bill got a shock; his bike was not parked in the street His prized possession had been stolen!

Bill looked around in disbelief. He remembered having gone out for extra booze and, when he came back, parking the bike outside the front gate. Although he was quite drunk this was sobering him up considerably. He walked around the block of houses hoping he had parked the bike opposite the wrong gate, but to no avail. He went back into the house and told the host his story; the host was very sympathetic and said that Bill should report it to the police. It would be best to report it tomorrow though, as they might smell alcohol on his breath and he would be locked up. Bill was offered a bed and, after several cups of coffee, he lay down to try to sleep. He could not sleep, rehashing the whole night and his ride on the bike. Obviously, he had not immobilized it. He kept thinking, why my bike, why me?

The next day he went home to collect the papers and then to the police station. He was having trouble explaining his loss to the policemen and cursing himself for not learning a bit more Arabic. Finally, an officer arrived who could speak English; he asked for the papers and said Bill should get photocopies as papers could get 'lost'. After Bill gave his statement the officer sympathized but did not inspire any confidence that the police would find the bike. Bill was almost in tears and the officer sat him down and ordered some tea. Tea was not going to solve Bill's problem, but he kept his thoughts to himself and drank the tea.

Bill left the police station and got a taxi to the Sudan Club. He wanted to get drunk but knew there was nothing in the club, but it was an oasis where he could collect his thoughts. He was still in a daze when he wandered into the lounge and drank a soft drink. The club was almost deserted, and he was glad because all he could do was to sit and stare at the wall. Some instinct told him to check the mailboxes where members received their mail. There was a letter for him; it was from Angela. He almost annihilated the envelope in his haste to get it open. The letter was the final blow. Angela did not want to see him again; she had met another man and was getting engaged soon. Bill could not finish the letter; the tears in his eyes made that impossible. He sat in the chair sobbing and thinking about ending his life. Someone came into the lounge, so he rushed out to the toilet. He sat for a long time and felt like vomiting, but nothing would come. Finally, he shakily left the club and caught a taxi home. All the way he looked at every motorcycle hoping that he would see his bike. His bike was unique, and he could spot it anywhere.

Back in the flat he stripped off to his underwear and flopped on the bed; he wanted to sleep but could not due to his visions of his bike and Angela. He got up to have a drink of water and tried to reread Angela's letter, but again tears stopped him getting to the end. The night passed with no sleep, but he was weary. The next day he could not go to work and when the foreman knocked on his door, he claimed he was sick. After two days he decided to go to work tell the whole story and ask the workers to look for his bike. Wahib was sympathetic, everyone was sympathetic, but that did not help. That evening he got hold of a bottle of Aragi and got drunk. That did not help either and just made him angry and full of self-pity.

After a few days the police came to his work and asked if he had found his bike. Luckily, he was sober and did not say what he was thinking. The work was being carried by the foreman, as Bill was always angry and insulting to the workers. Each night he got drunk and that did not help but only made him worse.

One morning, a driver came to the workshop with a letter sent by the fellow who had held the party. The letter was like a miracle. Bill's bike had been seen at a house in Khartoum North and the driver would take him there. Bill dropped everything and without a word to the foreman jumped into the car. The driver explained that he had been in North Khartoum and the traffic had been bad, so he had taken a short cut through some backstreets and he had spotted the bike, which he had seen many times before. Today the traffic was bad too and the ride seemed to take an interminable time to get to the house. The bike was not there, but the driver explained that he had seen it at about three p.m. the previous day, standing by the gate. Bill decided it was too long a wait till the afternoon, so he asked to be driven to the Sudan Club. He would come back later, what else could he do?

At about three p.m. he took a taxi and directed the driver to the house in Khartoum North. When he had been riding his bike, he had found Khartoum North a good place to buy booze, so he knew the area fairly well. They arrived at the house and there was his bike. His first impulse was to get on and ride away, but he wanted revenge. Bill was elated but he had to think clearly, so he got out of the taxi and to the amazement of the driver just removed the spark plug cable. Jumping back in the taxi he told the driver to take him to the police station. The driver seemed bemused but drove him to Khartoum North police station.

For the next half hour Bill tried to explain his problem. The police knew less English than the ones in Khartoum. Bill was trying to keep his temper but finally he persuaded two policemen to accompany him in the taxi. Bill was getting a bit desperate as he thought the bike might be moved. When they arrived at the house, Bill was elated to see the bike still there and a young man trying to start it. The man looked to be about twenty with long bushy hair, wearing dirty jeans and a faded blue shirt. The police spoke to him and an argument ensued. The taxi driver knew a little English and was explaining that the youth was claiming the bike was his. Suddenly the argument was over, and the police grabbed the youth and bundled him into the taxi. With the help of the taxi driver he explained to the police that he would ride the bike to the station. He also said he would pay the taxi driver at the station; this was an important point as the driver was getting anxious about the fare. The youth was shouting loudly, and a crowd gathered in the street but they stood back as the taxi and Bill drove away.

When Bill arrived at the station the youth was already behind bars and an officer had arrived. Bill had taken a detour to enjoy the ride and was glad to see an officer who spoke some English. Apparently the two policemen had arrested the young man because he had abused them but they were not sure about the stolen bike. Bill told the officer that all the paperwork was in the police station in Khartoum New Extension and was told by the officer that they would have to be transferred to Khartoum North as the suspect was now under their jurisdiction. The next bit of news put a significant damper on Bill's elation: the bike would have to stay in the compound as it was evidence for the trial. Bill must have shown his disappointment as the officer said, "Don't worry, under Sharia law justice is swift."

Bill took his leave and said goodbye to his bike after removing a couple of vital parts; he envisioned policemen driving around the yard on his prized possession. Later Bill arrived with the evidence of ownership and the officer waved the documents in front of the young man, who was still claiming the bike was his. Bill thought the youth must be mad, but he had no sympathy. He wanted revenge. When Bill left the station, he was pleased to hear that the preliminary hearing would be the next morning.

Bill was almost back to normal at work during the next couple of days, and everyone was pleased that the thief had been caught until a policeman arrived to see Bill. He was shown to Bill's office by the foreman. Bill's office was a dirty little room with a desk and two chairs and a calendar showing a couple of camels grazing (not a couple of sultry maidens). The foreman stood by the door in case there had to be some translation. The officer was pleased that the hearing had gone well and the youth had confessed to stealing the bike. The trial would be in a few days and there was only one problem. The youth was sure to be convicted and under Sharia law the wronged party had some say in the punishment. It was possible that the young man's right hand would be amputated, but if Bill did not want that the youth could get a long sentence. Without hesitation Bill said whatever the court decided he would agree to, but his preference was to have the hand chopped off. The officer was taken aback, and the foreman looked as if someone had just died. The officer said, "Are you sure that is what you want?"

Bill was looking angry and said, "After the problems this man has caused me, I see no reason why I should be lenient. He even had the gall to keep repeating that the bike was his when he was arrested. Chop the hand off." With that, the officer left, but he was visibly upset. The foreman, who was a Copt like Wahib, entered the office and pleaded with Bill to reconsider.

"You are a Christian like me, this law is barbaric, how can you do such a thing?" Bill just shrugged his shoulders and smiled; the foreman winced and left.

Later when Bill was walking around the factory, one of the workers came to Bill and said, "I am a Muslim and I like some parts of Sharia but I also believe in mercy. Please spare this young man; it will curse him for life."

Bill answered, "It is your law. It is the law of Sudan." In the afternoon Wahib came to the factory and was filled in on what had happened by the foreman. A sullen-faced Wahib entered Bill's office and said that the foremen had told him the story. "Do you know what you are doing to this young man? He may be a thief, but this punishment is too cruel. You can't do this."

"I can and I will," Bill answered resolutely.

"You are a Christian, this law is barbaric."

"It is your law. It is Sudanese law and I am allowing a thief to get his due punishment."

"It is not my law," blurted out Wahib going red in the face and accentuating the word 'my'. With that Wahib stormed out of the office.

Bill spent the evening riding in a taxi around Khartoum looking for people with their right hand missing. He now had a morbid interest in amputations but, as Sharia had not been in force for long, his search was unsuccessful. Several people's hands had been amputated and there was one double amputation (the right hand and the left leg below the knee) but Bill did not see them around Khartoum.

The next day at work an older man in a jalobia and emma (a white turban) and a woman in a tobe came to Bill's office. They were the young man's parents; Wahib had picked them up and brought them to the factory. The man spoke softly but in very good English. He was pleading mercy for his son, Abdul, who was not too bright and had been very foolish. "The law is too harsh," he said.

Bill said quite casually, "You are Muslim, and this is Muslim law and thieves must be punished."

"Yes, Sharia is God's law, but mercy is also in our teachings. This punishment is for someone who breaks into your house and steals, not for taking something left out in a public street." This annoyed Bill but he kept repeating that it was Sudanese law and the court would decide the punishment.

The woman was crying all the time and kept repeating, "Please, please." This had no effect on Bill, quite the reverse, he thought of Angela and how she had let him down and that made him more resolute. Finally, the couple left with Wahib and Bill settled down behind his desk. A group of workers came to the office to plead the case, but Bill told them to get back to work in rather impolite terms.

Bill did not have to attend the court but he wanted to be there. He watched the proceedings, much of which he did not comprehend, but he could see the parents in tears pleading for mercy. The trial was very quickly over and there was a gasp from the audience when the verdict was pronounced. The police officer came to Bill and explained the verdict and asked Bill whether he would like to show leniency, but Bill was more confident in his decision. Bill's only interest was to get his bike back and, after the paperwork was completed, he might get it back the next day. After the police officer left a well-dressed Sudanese sat beside Bill. This man was dressed in a suit with a tie and spoke in an educated English tone. He explained to Bill that as Sharia had only been in force for a short time the judges were handing down severe sentences and the crime committed did not deserve a hand amputation. Bill was unmoved.

Bill was elated to be able to recover his bike, and he rode away the next day with all the paperwork and no apparent damage to the bike. Wahib was not so happy and he started to get angry with Bill and pushier about work. The foreman and the workers became sullen and unhelpful and seemed to avoid him when he went to the factory floor. On the day of Abdul's amputation Bill arrived to a deserted factory with a crude note on his door: No Work Today! At last Bill started to think about what he had done but he had not decided the penalty and, after all, this bloke had caused him lots of grief.

The news leaked out into the expatriate community and members at the club started to shun him. One day John came to the club and approached Bill. "Did you have a man's hand amputated for stealing your bike?" Bill answered very quietly in the affirmative; he was now starting to regret his decision. "That is barbaric. How could you do it? I can't understand your thinking; would you have done that in the UK?"

"The man stole my bike and was convicted in 'his' court and the sentence was amputation."

"I agree, but you had the chance to change the sentence. If you believe in this law as you say you break it every day by drinking illicit booze. You are a hypocrite." With that John walked quickly away leaving Bill open mouthed.

After that altercation with John, Bill descended into a period of critical reflection. Did he do right? He then started to think about all the problem it had caused him, all the money spent on taxis, all the time he had tried to explain the problem to the police, all the time he had not been able to use his bike. Yes, he was right! He still had the problem that everywhere he looked there seemed to be eyes looking and criticizing him though. The Sudan Club became a lonely place and even the manager and the gate guard seemed to avoid him. At work no one spoke to him unless they had to and the workers all seemed to be looking at him, but when he looked back, they turned their heads. In his flat he started drinking heavily again; even his neighbours seemed to avoid him.

Bill was actually doing more work now and Wahib was bringing in work but was very curt with Bill. One day Wahib came to Bill's office and announced that business was bad, and he would have to let Bill go. This was a big shock to Bill as he thought business was getting better. The next shock was that Wahib presented Bill with unpaid bills. There were customs and clearing of his bike, transport for the bike, Sudan Club fees and the fifty-pound loan from when Bill arrived. Bill was initially speechless but when he could respond he could only say, "I can't pay."

Wahib looked Bill straight in the eye and said quite coldly, "Sell me the bike, then you will have some pounds to take home. I have already bought your air ticket." Bill was so shocked he could not reply; he had tears in his eyes and a lump in his throat. "It is the only way. Your time in Sudan has come to an end."

Bill went home and lay on the bed thinking about all his problems. He was going to lose his bike, he was losing his job and he would only have a few pounds when he arrived back in the UK. Angela would not be waiting! This whole trip had been a disaster, what had he done wrong? A bottle of Aragi helped him decide that the only way was out. He wanted to get back to England and hoped it was raining to wash the dust off his face. Now he hated Khartoum, everything and everyone was against him here and he wanted out.

The next day Wahib asked Bill for his decision and Bill just gave over the papers for the bike, Bill did not even negotiate a price; he just wanted to leave. Wahib handed Bill the air ticket and promised him some sterling the next day, As Wahib was about to leave Bill dejectedly asked, "What are you going to do with the bike?"

"Give it to Ahmed's family."

An Unfortunate Insult

John had graduated with a degree in engineering, civil engineering; he worked for a company with many contracts at home and abroad. With the company he had had several jobs in the UK, when the management secured a large construction job in Tanzania. John was a little reluctant to go to Tanzania, but the salary was too good for him to refuse. He found Tanzania challenging; his first time in Africa made him aware of the difference in lifestyle and pace of life. While adjusting to life he found the expatriate community and made friends from various countries. A lot of his friends had boats and he learned to sail. He enjoyed sailing out of Dar Es Salaam and even sailed to Zanzibar with some English friends. After the Tanzanian job he was sent to South Africa, where he enjoyed his job and the country. He worked with South Africans, both black and white, and enjoyed their company. In some ways he mixed more with the locals there than he had in Tanzania. Unfortunately, the job finished quickly and he was soon on his way to Zimbabwe. This was the first time he found work and the conditions really difficult and frustrating, so he asked for a transfer. He really noticed that the poverty in Zimbabwe was disturbing him. The best job offered by the company was in Khartoum, where he would be a general manager. The conditions and pay were very good and replies to his enquiries of friends within the company, were positive.

John arrived in Khartoum a seasoned hand in Africa. The airport was definitely the worst he had seen but the officials and people were polite and helpful. His passage through the airport was swift and efficient. He was assured by the company staff that his baggage would be cleared and delivered to him in a couple of hours. He was whisked away in a company car to his new residence. This was a fully furnished three-bedroom house with a swimming pool. He had a cook, a cleaner, a driver and day and night guards, all paid for by the company. There was a large generator in case of power cuts and an old Land Rover for visiting the more remote locations. There was also an air-conditioned car for around Khartoum. The set-up was really for a married man although he was a bachelor.

His main office was near the centre of town but there were offices at the three construction sites under his control. The CEO was a Sudanese, who was a partner with the parent company John worked for. The house where he would live was owned by the CEO's brother and he later found that many of the clerical staff were related to the CEO too. All the sites had an expatriate supervisor with the rest of the work crew being Sudanese.

After a good night's sleep, he was awoken by the cook who asked what he would like for breakfast. They had no bacon, so he settled for eggs on toast. He had never been treated so well in his other jobs and thought there must be a catch. His breakfast was washed down with a delicious fruit juice. He quizzed the cook and found that he had been trained by the British during colonial times. The cook had a whole list of English dishes he could cook, including roast beef and Yorkshire pudding and shepherd's pie. Bacon and pork were hard to get and he preferred not to cook them on religious grounds and he warned John that the local sausages were not up to English standards. John was impressed and said so, much to the delight of the cook. The driver arrived and said that John should go to the office to meet the CEO. On reaching the office he was greeted by a tall man in a flowing white gown who introduced himself as Said. Said's English was very good and they had a long discussion about work and the locations of the works, interrupted several times by small glasses of tea. Said said, that the running of the company was up to John; Said would only come into the picture if there were new jobs or problems with the government. Said had other businesses to run and, although it was his biggest venture, this was not in his realm of expertise. Before Said left, John was introduced to the office staff and shown a map of the site locations.

John thought that he should take a look around Khartoum, so he took one of the office staff for a ride. The first place to see was the Sudan Club which was within walking distance of the office. They then drove along the Nile past the palace, university and an open-air cinema. They doubled back and saw the ferry to Tuti Island and the museum. Their drive took them along the Nile till they crossed a bridge to Omdurman. The traffic was quite heavy on the bridge as there was a police checkpoint. They were stopping cars and buses, but John's car was waved through and they drove to the souk and then towards the desert. The souk looked like many African markets he had seen, except that his guide told him on Fridays there would be Dervishes dancing. Out towards the desert, John had expected to see camels but all he saw were lots of goats and carts pulled by donkeys. The road along the Nile was interesting and then they crossed another bridge leading to North Khartoum.

North Khartoum seemed to be less populated and, on that day, had much less traffic. One very interesting place was a cricket club near the bridge to Khartoum. The guide did not know much about cricket but he had a relative who had played in England. This relative had taken him to watch a game but he could not understand the rules. John smiled, as the rules of cricket seemed to be unknown to most of the world. Near the cricket ground was a dairy and this was to be the first and only time John saw cows in Khartoum. Another place close to the Nile was the Soba Prison, a place that he would see a nasty sight in the future. After crossing the bridge into Khartoum, they drove along a road almost parallel to the airport runway. The road took them to the end of the runway and then joined another road running at right angles into the main residential area of Khartoum.

John's impression was that the three cities were not attractive, being mainly one- and two-storey houses, often enclosed by mud brick walls. All the buildings were a sandy colour with few having much paint left on them. The only attractive parts were along the Nile, but two places registered as places to investigate, the Sudan Club and the cricket club.

His first visit to a construction site was near a newly built power station in Khartoum North. The driver advised that they could go by car but that the road near the site was rough and littered with broken glass, so they should take the Land Rover. John was getting used to the air-conditioned car, which the Land Rover did not have and the road was dusty, demanding that they keep the windows almost shut. He was glad to get into the site office. This was the first time he had really been affected the dry heat of Khartoum. After several glasses of cold water, he was able to talk to the site manager, a German who had been in Sudan many years.

The schedule of work had been mapped out by the previous general manager and it was a little optimistic. Otto explained that the workers had initially been very slow but they were improving. He had stressed to them that unless their work rate improved, they would be replaced. Otto admitted that this was an idle threat as he could not foresee getting a better gang of workers. John was impressed with Otto and as he walked around the site, all he could see were smiling faces. Maybe Otto had told them that John had come to see if they needed a new gang.

After that first site visit John was keen to see the Sudan Club. Khartoum was severely lacking entertainment. There were a few hotels with bars, an open-air cinema along the Nile but little else. As Friday was the day off, he went straight to the Sudan Club. The gate boy was insistent that John be signed in as a guest, this was the first time a Sudanese had told him what he should do, and he was impressed. The gate boy pointed out the bar where he would surely find someone to sign him into the club. It was well before noon and the bar was full with members enjoying their first, second or third beers and was very noisy. John introduced himself to a young man sitting at the bar with a young lady and asked if they would sign him in as a guest. They were very happy to meet him and duly signed him into the club. The couple were both employed at the embassy and they were at the club for the Friday lunch, which was roast beef and Yorkshire pudding, the best in town. John was advised that the office was closed and if he wished to join the club he should come back tomorrow.

John enjoyed his first day at the club. He stayed for the lunch and was planning to test out his cook in the preparation of roast beef. It was the first time he had tried the local beer called Camel and, although he was not a big beer drinker, it compared well with other beers he had drunk in Africa. As he left, he realized that all he had seen of the club was the bar and the restaurant; he would have to investigate the rest on Saturday.

Saturday turned out to be not such a good day, as he had to go out to a site south of Khartoum. The road was rough and not far along they got a puncture. Although early morning, it was very hot and after jacking up the Land Rover the wheel would not come off. The driver said he would get help and left John guarding the car. Fortunately, John had brought a bottle of water with him but that disappeared very fast. Having nothing to do John tried a couple of times to remove the wheel but not one nut would budge. As he sat there in the shade of the car a couple of men seemed to come from nowhere; they greeted him and carried on their way oblivious of his dilemma. John was bemused but his lack of Arabic had not allowed him to explain his predicament; he vowed to learn some basic Arabic.

What seemed to be hours elapsed before he could see a taxi approaching along the track. John's driver got out and explained that John should take the taxi back home and he would wait for the mechanics. The taxi was an old Morris Minor that had seen better days. The windscreen had a large crack, the rear door would not shut properly and there was only one window winder handle. John was so thirsty he told his driver to tell the taxi driver to stop at the first stall where he could get bottled water or soft drinks. The track had been rough in the Land Rover but in the taxi, he bounced around continuously. He wondered whether the taxi would make it to the main road. They did make the main road and stopped at a stall selling soft drinks, which were not very cold but very welcome. John bought several bottles and gave one to the taxi driver, who thanked him in broken English.

Finally, they reached his house, and John paid the taxi driver what was asked without haggling. John was so glad to get into somewhere with air conditioning and have a cool shower. He lay on the bed and felt dizzy, much later he awoke with a splitting headache and he was nauseous. He did not realize at the time that he had sun stroke.

Late in the afternoon the Land Rover came back. The driver explained that it had taken several men to remove the wheel and replace it with the spare. He had driven them to the office so they could get paid and they were so happy they were going to spend the night in Khartoum. John took in most of the information but he was in no state to comprehend everything. He did resolve to have all the wheels of their vehicles checked so that this could not happen again. There was no Saturday night for John at the club.

John met Said on the Sunday and told him of his adventure; Said smiled. He diagnosed John with sun stroke and he advised John to always have a hat and plenty of water. Even in a Land Rover many of those tracks could be so rutted that only lorries with a high clearance could make the journey. The driver had taken the shortest route to the site, but supply trucks took a longer route on slightly better roads. Said had a trucking company and knew almost all the mechanics in the area, who specialized in fixing broken-down trucks and could remove any wheel. Said was sympathetic but told John that in the Sudan things could be tough but inshallah everything would work out. John was to learn that most Sudanese, whether religious or not, had a calm feeling that God would extract them from difficulty. This so contrasted with the locals he had met in Zimbabwe.

The Sudan Club became his regular haunt; he enjoyed the food (his cook could not get Yorkshire pudding quite right), the pool was better than his and the snooker room was his favourite place. He realized that the beauty of the restaurant was the company of members, so he started to have a weekly dinner party at his place. Said was invited and, although he did not drink, enjoyed the company, as he was ever on the lookout for new business. At one of the parties John said that Said should bring his wife the next time. Said's reply was that John should meet his wife first. That set John's imagination running as Said's reply was not what he had expected.

John was invited to Said's house for dinner; there would be no other guests and no alcohol. John asked whether he could bring anything and the answer was no, that guests should only bring themselves. John decided that Said's place would be air conditioned and so no shorts, no sandals; slacks and a short-sleeved shirt would seem appropriate. Actually, John was unsure what to expect; he had not formally met a Sudanese woman. Said greeted him at the front gate and they entered a very nicely furnished lounge with a marble floor, two large chairs and two large settees. Said ushered John into a chair and said that his wife spoke perfect English and understood a lot about English politics. Not my strong suit thought John.

Into the room came a beautiful woman, quite tall and wearing a long gown covered with a brightly covered tobe, which covered her head and shoulders. She was obviously much younger than Said. She introduced herself as Jasmina and shook John's hand. She sat in the chair facing John forcing Said to sit on the settee. After a few pleasantries she asked John's opinion of Sudan. John told her of his site visits, the Sudan Club and how he thought most Sudanese to be more relaxed than other Africans he had met. He asked whether she had been to the UK; he had asked the right question. She answered that she had been to England several times and loved every place she had visited. London was very impressive but with too many people; Oxford was so full of history she would love to spend more time there and York was so relaxed but also impressive.

"I am originally from York, although of course I lived in the suburbs," replied John.

"Did you go to university in York?"

"No, I went to Birmingham University."

"I have also been to Birmingham and seen the university tower with the clock."

John started to realize that Jasmina knew more about England than he could remember. Somehow the discussion got onto politics and John was way out of his depth. Emily Pankhurst was a favourite of Jasmina, but when her name was mentioned Said started to frown, although he had been smiling and silent through the rest of the discussion. John was reluctant but decided to ask.

"How do you know all this?"

Jasmina laughed and said, "You have asked the right question. When I went to Khartoum University to study English, we had lecturers from England. One of them taught us English History and Literature. He was always talking about 'then and now' and contrasting and comparing the past, present and future. History and Literature can be dry but when you start to see similarities and contrasts with the past it become bright and enlightening."

What a woman, thought John, as Jasmina excused herself to see to the children. As she left, she invited him to come to their home anytime he wished. Said smiled and waited till his wife had left the room and then apologised for his wife dominating the conversation.

John said, "No apologies needed. That was the most enlightening hour I have spent in the Sudan. You ought to take her to talk to the ambassador; he is a history buff."

Said explained that he was a simple trader and his wife was more educated than he and she was well worth the dowry he had paid. She kept a very good house and when his friends came, she entertained the wives in a separate room, but he could not let her loose on the male company. Occasionally foreign visitors would let her 'get rid of heat' as he put it, and John had been one of the recipients. John and Said became very close friends and John visited Said at least once a month.

The membership of the Sudan Club introduced John to the cricket club. Games at the club were often played on Friday, sometimes on Saturday afternoon and occasionally on Sunday afternoon. John was not much of a cricketer but went when he could for the company of like-minded idiots playing cricket in forty-degree heat. He took Said to the cricket and Said thought this game was too complicated, but when Said met a fellow Sudanese who had factories in the south and north of Sudan, Said was hooked. The fellow Sudanese was a Copt who had gone to boarding school in England and was very good with the bat. Said thanked John for the introduction but professed that cricket was not for him. After the cricket there were, of course, refreshments, mainly beer as the bar was well stocked.

John was invited to join the darts club which took place at the cricket club and in members' houses. John obtained a dart board and set up a room to invite darts teams to his house. Darts was fun and with teams of three and their 'supporters', generally wives, this was a good night. The teams were often mixed and when John invited Said to one of the games, he was astounded that women could throw darts. Outside work, the Sudan Club, cricket and darts occupied John's spare time and he loved this posting.

It was about 1980 when someone suggested that they have a hare and hounds type event called the Hash House Harriers. A trail and false trails would be set and the 'pack' would follow and find the end of the trail. John was sceptical; in this heat, who would run? John helped organize the first run though, and he was hooked. Two members would set the trail with lots of false trails and about half an hour later the pack would follow. The keen runners would go ahead and the slower pack would follow, collecting at a divergent path point. When the correct path was found the pack would proceed. Initially every runner was male and all expatriates. John thought that in this heat this sport was a non-starter but after about the second run wives started joining and visiting children started to run. After the run lots of liquid was consumed, mainly beer. John was hooked and he joined in, generally taking part as the back marker, ostensibly so that no one got lost but in reality, because he was a poor runner and enjoyed a walk now and then.

After the run there were lots of drinks and songs, starting with 'Swing Low Sweet Chariot' with all its weird symbolism. John loved this bit of England, even though many of the members were Australians, Canadians, Americans and South Africans. Due to the heat, the first beer went down 'without touching the sides'. During the post-run celebrations some poor individual who had made a mistake had to do a 'down-down' which was drinking a pint of some liquid, generally beer, in one go, then putting the upturned glass on one's head. This was not limited to men, but spilt cold beer on a hot body was not unpleasant.

Suddenly Sharia descended on the Sudan, on a Saturday morning. This was to change the Sudan, particularly for the expatriates. John was in the office early and, as they drove to the centre of Khartoum he had seen many soldiers on the street but thought nothing of it. He was drinking his first glass of tea when the driver came into the office; he was excited.

"Nimeri has declared Sharia, we will have God's law."

"What does that mean?" said John.

"I am not sure, but it must be good."

John had arrived at the office early and had to wait until some of his more educated staff appeared. His secretary had some information, "The army are unloading the beer stores and they say they will throw the contents into the Nile. There are crowds gathering and the army are out in force. They have closed several roads and are trying to disperse the crowds; don't go out yet."

John had not planned to leave the office as he was awaiting the arrival of Said for a review of the projects they were working on. John decided to shut himself off from the excitement in the office as this news was all confusing. Finally Said arrived and after a few pleasantries they sat alone in John's office to discuss the situation.

"I think the announcement was made last night although I did not hear the speech. Apparently, Sharia is to be the law of the whole country, but what form of Sharia I am not sure. I suggest you take the day off and come to my house tomorrow morning. I will try to get more information and we can discuss how it will affect our business," said Said. John gave a weak smile; Said was always thinking of business.

Early on Sunday morning John arrived at Said's house to be greeted by Jasmina. "Technically we should not be seen together in the absence of my husband, so let us go quickly in doors." John was bemused but entered the house quickly. "Said will be back soon. He is consulting some friends in the government. I assume you have many questions but as yet we do not have all the answers. What we know is that this law is to cover the whole of Sudan, but in the south, there are many Christians and I fear that could be a problem. The law will be welcomed by many Sudanese as it should cut down on robbery and petty theft, but how it will affect expatriates like you we are yet to find out." John listened to this devout Muslim woman who seemed as confused as he.

Finally Said arrived and the news was not good.

"This is a full implementation of Sharia law; it affects all Sudanese, residents and even tourists. Alcohol is completely banned; anyone smelling of liquor can expect twenty-five lashes. There are severe penalties for robbery including amputations. Adultery and homosexuality are to be severely punished. The banking system has to change to conform to Sharia law. Business is not really affected as far as I can tell."

"Surely this does not apply to me."

"Of course it does. When you are in a country you have to obey the laws of that country," Jasmina said sharply.

Later when John went to the Sudan Club, he found that the bar was closed and the booze locked up. The cricket club closed its bar and henceforth they struggled to get two teams to play a game on Friday or Saturday afternoon. Darts still carried on in people's houses but the enthusiasm for the sport waned with little or no booze available. The Hash continued but with very few numbers. One organization was born though, the KGB. The Khartoum Guild of Brewers was formed when expatriates started to brew their own beer and wine (which was illegal of course). At first the products of these endeavours were pretty terrible, or as one expat put it 'taste bud bashing'. However, the quality began to improve as beer kits started to be smuggled into

Khartoum. The wine was very variable but could be quite tasty; grapes were not plentiful or cheap, but raisons and sultanas made passable wines. John held one or two wine and beer tasting events, although he always seemed to be able to source small amounts of real stuff.

The expatriate numbers dwindled slightly, but there was not the mass exodus predicted by some expats. John continued to use the Sudan Club for lunch; the pool and snooker room were still popular. Leaving his office, which could be quite crowded and loud, he could stroll down the chaos of the main street and then enter a quiet orderly place where he could relax. If everything in the office was going well, he would often spend half of the afternoon in the club. The embassy had a club for its staff and he was occasionally invited there, but he disliked the atmosphere. Most of the embassy staff moaned about accommodation and pay, although they received a hardship allowance.

John still had parties in his house and as the KGB got more organized and the product improved there was about one party a week. The participants had to be careful of being stopped by the police so there were many more lady drivers than before. At one of John's parties a participant had his motorbike stolen, and John had to put the guest up for the night so he could report to the police in a sober state. Even the Hash started to pick up again with some runners taking their own refreshments, but John decided that he would abstain until he reached home.

After several months of Sharia, life settled back to almost normal. The south of Sudan had been largely exempted from Sharia and after an initial flurry of amputations the robbery rate had decreased, and people became more accustomed to the limitations. Said had sorted out his banking problems and work on the three sites was progressing smoothly. Said was always keen for John to entertain guest of the associated companies and also those he was trying to involve in his empire. A couple who were going to Kenya came to stay for a week; no parties were planned and, after showing them around Khartoum, the only event was a Hash run. They were both younger than John and keen to run on the Hash, but John was less enthusiastic and decided not to run that day.

After the run and the usual formalities John and his guests climbed into the Land Rover. John had decided to use the Land Rover as the running terrain was on the outskirts of south Khartoum and the roads were rough. They reached the tarmac road and had gone about a mile when suddenly a car came out of the desert straight across the path of the Land Rover. Both cars swerved and ended up off the road in the desert. John had applied the brakes and his female passenger in the back had hit an unyielding metal strut with her knee. On seeing the blood John dashed out of his car and started banging on the roof of the other car. Normally John was a very relaxed individual but this accident had scared him and made him angry. He was calling the driver a bloody idiot and lots of other names. The driver seemed to be in a daze but after a while climbed out of his car. That was when John realized he was a senior police officer. The pips on his lapel and the braid around his cap confirmed John's opinion. John was still mad and took down the number plate of the car in his notebook.

"You cannot do that," said the officer, when he finally spoke. "This is a police security car." As soon as John heard the word security, he knew he had a problem. Before he could react, a bus full of policemen pulled off the road. The officer gave a command in Arabic which John could not translate but understood that he was being arrested. John quickly told his guests to take the Land Rover to his house and contact Said.

The police bus took John to Khartoum police station where he sat while someone wrote a page of notes that he could not read He was presented with a charge in Arabic and asked to sign. John explained that he could not read Arabic and refused to sign. They then took him to a cell and demanded his shoes; he refused to give the shoes, but they were satisfied when he gave them the laces. John did not understand the significance of the shoes or the laces, but he was glad he had kept his shoes when he entered the cell. It was occupied by several men; the floor was wet and the smell almost overpowering. There was much amusement by his cellmates, but he was allowed to sit by the bars of the doors to get some fresh air.

After about two hours Said showed up at the station. John was let out and Said took him home. John was told to stay at home and that Said would see the chief of police in the morning. John was glad to see his visitors and related his experiences; the lady had a large plaster on her leg but seemed OK. They all had a large drink and mulled over the day's happenings.

The next morning Said came with a serious face. "Unfortunately, you abused the third in command of the Sudan Police Force and he wants to press charges. You have two witnesses, but they are leaving for Kenya tomorrow. With the chaotic state of the courts we cannot let this go to trial; you may have to spend time in jail and that is not a good option. You should pack and I will get you on a flight tonight. I will pick you up tonight and take you to the airport."

John was taken aback but no way did he want to spend time in Soba Prison. As he packed, he was regretting leaving the best job he had ever had. He was sure he would get another posting, but a moment of anger and verbal abuse had cost him a lot. Said picked him up in the evening and brought Jasmina along to say goodbye. She thought that John was probably in the right, but he could be used as an example of the indiscipline of the foreigner. They said goodbyes and promised to meet up in the UK.

On the plane to the UK John could only think of two things. Jasmina's statement — when you are in a country you have to obey the laws of that country. The second was that you have to be careful who you insult when not in your own country.

Getting the Bumps Knocked Out

The time is fast approaching when I will be leaving Khartoum, probably for good. Africa gets in your blood and perhaps I will return one day maybe even to Khartoum. They say that once you have tasted Nile water you will return. I have mixed emotions about leaving but I know I have had enough, at least for a while. Having lived here for six years, I think Sudan is on a slow slide downwards. I have a lot of junk to offload and, although my car is not exactly junk, it has outlived its usefulness. I want to sell the car for a decent price, so I am trying to make my vehicle look as good as possible.

My car is a 1976 Hillman Avenger with air conditioning which could never keep pace with Khartoum heat. It's old and has seen better days but it runs quite well and probably will do so for many years. I am in the Omdurman Industrial area getting the bumps knocked out, before selling the car. Omdurman is on the other side of the Nile from Khartoum and the industrial area is on the western outskirts of Omdurman. This is an area the Mahdi would have known well and that nomads with their camels would frequent when they came to the big city. I saw a couple of camels on my drive here; they seemed to be grazing although I could not see anything edible near them. To get here I had to drive over unsurfaced roads, really just desert tracks.

I was recommended this place by a Sudanese friend who had given me a roughly drawn map. I almost turned back at one stage though, the place looked so bleak. The mechanics have offered me a seat in the shade, a crudely fashioned stool which after a while is hard on my backside. The shade is very welcome, and my position is ideal for watching the activity around me. I am trying to take in all the sights, sounds and smells. I must be leaving Sudan soon, so I am trying to take in everything so I can remember it.

The main focus of my attention is the boy rubbing down the paint work where they bashed out the bumps. He looks about sixteen years of age although he could be anywhere between fourteen and twenty. He has a dirty blue and white cap turned backwards like a baseball player. He has a ragged once-white shirt buttoned only in one place. I don't think there is another button on it. The sleeves are neatly rolled up to reveal his dark brown almost skinny arms. His arms are shiny, hairless, not exactly muscular, wirier; the veins stick out. On his right wrist is a black elephant hair bangle. He has baggy grey-blue trousers that seem to hang awkwardly on his slim body. The bottoms are frayed and dragging on the ground. The fly seems to be held together with a couple of safety pins. There still appears to be a semblance of a crease down both legs which seems amazing considering the age of the trousers and their harsh treatment. Faded yellow flip-flops adorn his dusty feet and his big flat heels make a lasting impression on my mind. There is an intent expression on his face as he moves back and forth rubbing down the wing of my car.

I look around at what surrounds me. Before coming to Africa, I would have described this place as extremely filthy or words to that effect. Now I am more sympathetic; I have seen worse. This is the edge of the desert and a place of crude industry; it is a poor area but a place where all ages can make a living. It is to me a friendly place where I can see people treating others with respect but to me there is special respect. I am hawadja, the foreigner, probably the only one in this area at the time. I have white in my beard and so I am an older man and as such I command respect unless I prove myself unworthy of it. Of course when it comes to paying the bill it will be every man for himself and there will be a lot of hard bargaining. I might be able to reduce the price but even for an expatriate I am a poor haggler. It is a skill I don't have mainly because it takes patience and time and in this heat I have neither.

Sitting here in the street I am observing but also being observed. I get smiles, shy looks and the occasional Arabic greeting from passers-by; I have not seen a woman in this area. After a few minutes one man comes out of the next shop for a chat. He is an older man in a dirty jalobia who speaks quite good English. This rather fat, balding man has beautiful white teeth and an infectious smile. I warm to him and start to ask him questions.

He owns one of the spare part shops. I point to my Avenger and he shakes his head. He does not have parts for a Hillman; he stocks Toyota parts. A tea seller comes past and offers me a glass of tea but I decline. I would love a drink, but I have seen the water he uses to wash the glasses and it has been well used. My shopkeeper friend starts to point out the sights. The first thing he pointed out was a shop three doors down the street belonging to Abdul; that was the first; he might have some Hillman parts. I look down the sand track loosely called a street; it is dirty, dusty, oily, full of parts from a thousand cars and bits of rag everywhere. All the shops are similar to the one behind me giving me shade, they are crudely built one-room buildings made of mud and crude bricks topped with a corrugated iron roof. Many of the roofs are torn and twisted but not rusted. This dry climate of the Sudan saves a little of the ageing process but the sand makes everything else, especially the sparse paint work, look seedy. Inwardly I laugh when I think of the rusted roofs in some other African cities.

My talkative friend is called Hashim and he lives in Omdurman near the Nile. He was at school when they had some English teachers and that accounts for his quite good English. He starts to ask me about my Avenger. I tell him it is sold, a little white lie, although

I do have an offer. "Why do you need to fix your car? What is wrong with it?" he asks and I decide to tell him the story. I am interested to see his reaction.

I explain that I went to the Sudan Club (the British club) in Khartoum. I was going to play snooker with some friends. I parked my car in a street which ran along the side wall of the club. My car was parked facing the wall next to my friend's Hillman Avenger. All the cars were facing the wall and the people had to walk down the centre of the street. There was a small part of the wall where cars could not park due to a rubbish dump near the corner of the street. Most times it was just a sort of mound, occasionally there was a large metal bin but that always stank.

I am telling this to Hashim in as simple an English as I can and of course there is a lot of hand waving. I do not attempt to explain snooker; I just tell him snooker is an indoor game played by hawajas. Lots of Sudanese play card games and shish bish (a form of backgammon) but snooker would be unknown to them. Hashim says he has heard of the hawaja club and thinks he knows the street, although he goes to Khartoum very infrequently.

Halfway through the second game of snooker one of the guards came and called my friend Tony outside. After a few minutes Tony came back and excitedly told me to come and look at something he could not believe. I handed my cue to another player and hoped he would have better luck than I. I followed Tony outside and was temporarily blinded by the sun. After allowing my eyes to adjust I followed Tony out of the gate and around the corner into the street where our cars were parked. I could not believe my eyes. There was a brand-new Avenger interlocked with Tony's car which was interlocked with my car. The first two cars had obviously hit the wall but luckily my car had not moved so far. The wall was basically unscathed, but the two Avengers looked like write-offs.

I stared in disbelief and asked the obvious question, "What happened?" Tony was too shaken up to say anything but one of the Sudan Club gate boys told me the story in a pidgin English with lots of histrionics and sounds. The brand-new Avenger with no number plates had taken the corner at speed. The car had hit the rubbish dump, swerved across the road and then back again into Tony's car. The two cars hit the wall then Tony's car hit my car. Two men got out of the blue Avenger and were arrested by bystanders one of whom went to get a policeman. The men were taken away to jail with a large crowd following them.

Of course, the story was a lot lengthier than that and even though I was a little upset I was highly amused at the arm waving, sounds and explanations of the event. Tony later added a bit more to the story. The driver was a tall Dinka who admitted he had no licence and it was his first drive; he did this while smiling all the time. Tony was going back to the police station and would fill me in on more details later.

Some passers-by helped us pull the cars apart and I found that although my wing was well dented, it was not touching the wheel, and my car was perfectly drivable. Nothing else seemed to be damaged so I went back to the snooker game. The room was full of laughter when I told the story, followed by a quick exodus for a look. Two or three games and a few beers later Tony reappeared and filled us in on the rest of the story. The owner had been found and the car was brand new having been in Khartoum for just one day since delivery from Port Sudan. The car was not registered or insured, and the owner had been expecting a buyer that day. The Dinka was the owner's night watchman and had been given the keys so the potential buyer could look at the car. The Dinka's friend had arrived before the buyer and had been taken for a ride by a man who could not drive. Even the police seemed to think it was funny.

Tony's car was written off and so he had to claim on his insurance and, as his car had hit mine, I would have to as well. Even after sober reflection, I think I did the right thing in telling Tony not to bother with my claim. I drove Tony home and then got home and had a good laugh. The next day Tony got his police report and found that the Dinka was at the mercy of his boss and would stay in jail. Tony got his insurance money after a few months and bought another Avenger with the help of the blue Avenger owner. The Dinka stayed in jail for a few months and when let out was told to leave

Khartoum and go south. Here I was four years later having the bumps knocked out.

The incredible thing is that the Avenger was not a common car in the Sudan and having three of them locked together was probably unique. I finished the story and looked enquiringly at Hashim waiting for him to make a comment. He shook his head, smiled and said matter of factually, "In Khartoum it can happen."